THE LIFE AND TIMES OF BENNY ALVAREZ

ALSO BY PETER JOHNSON

FOR CHILDREN
The Amazing Adventures of John Smith, Jr. AKA Houdini

FOR TEENS
What Happened
Out of Eden
Loserville

THE **LIFE** AND **TIMES** OF **BENNY ALVAREZ**

PETER JOHNSON

HARPER
An Imprint of HarperCollinsPublishers

www.harpercollinschildrens.com

Library of Congress Cataloging-in-Publication Data
Johnson, Peter, date
    The life and times of Benny Alvarez / Peter Johnson. — First edition.
        pages   cm
    Summary: As his English teacher focuses on poetry during the month of
October, Benny faces down the smartest girl at school while also navigating
his friendships and a difficult family life after his grandfather's multiple strokes.
    ISBN 978-0-06-221596-3 (hardback)
    [1. Friendship—Fiction. 2. Poetry—Fiction. 3. Schools—Fiction. 4.
Family life—Fiction.]   I. Title.
PZ7.J6356Li   2014   2013043072
[Fic]—dc23   CIP
                                                                      AC

Typography by Michelle Gengaro-Kokmen
14 15 16 17 18   CG/RRDH   10 9 8 7 6 5 4 3 2 1
❖
First Edition

THIS ONE'S FOR LUCAS, MY BEST BUD

AS ALWAYS, THANKS TO PHOEBE FOR HER KEEN EDITORIAL EYE.
ALSO, A SHOUT-OUT TO LUCAS JOHNSON FOR HIS POEMS
"SUNGLASSES" AND "BALLOON."

THE LIFE AND TIMES OF BENNY ALVAREZ

THE GLASS-HALF-FULL-HALF-EMPTY EPISODE

First, a test:

Let's say you're cruising on your skateboard down a street you know better than the secret places where you stash forbidden sticks of gum or that red joy buzzer you trick your younger brother with, when out of nowhere a squirrel cuts you off, making you fall and break your ankle. Bad luck? Punishment for the times you lied to your parents or pranked your older sister? Or is it a sign to be prepared for the unexpected?

And when you're sitting at home watching old reruns of *Tom and Jerry* with your broken ankle resting on a chair while your best friend draws pictures of vampires on your cast, are you mad because your soccer season is as dead as a fly trapped between your front screen and picture window? Or do you look at the bright side and say, "Although my foot hurts worse than getting beat by a girl in arm wrestling, I could've broken my neck"?

"It's about the way you view the world" is what my mother would say, and what she's saying right now for the hundredth time. She's pointing to a half-full glass of water sitting on the kitchen table. The first time she used this expression, I looked up its definition in *Proteus: A Word Dictionary and Thesaurus for Children, with Explanations of Well-Known Phrases*, which me and my friends Beanie and Jocko just call the Book. I even memorized the entry: *The glass half empty or half full is a common expression used to determine the way someone views the world, whether someone is an optimist or a pessimist. That is, whether they see a glass with an even amount of water in it as being half full or half empty.*

I often wonder how long it takes my mother to perfectly measure the water. Does she tape a ruler to the outside of the glass, or follow a scientific formula, like the ones that confuse me on science exams, especially when they try to be funny: "If Beth has a gallon cereal bowl, and it's half filled with milk, will it still be half filled when she adds cereal?"

"Only a cow has a gallon cereal bowl," I complain to Ms. Butterfield, aka Ms. Demigoddess, or Ms. D for short, who's been strong-armed into proctoring my science exam. "Just take the test, Benny," she says.

But it's a trick question. Are we talking about oatmeal, Froot Loops, Cheerios? Are we talking about whole milk, 2 percent, or skim?

"Just take the test, Benny," Ms. D counters again with her excruciatingly pleasant (the Book would say "glorious") smile, a smile you can't say no to. Ms. D could tell you to stick your head in a toilet bowl for two minutes, and you'd gladly do it as long as she kept smiling. But back to the glass-half-full-half-empty episode.

There's something different about the glass today. When my mother asks me whether it's half full or half empty, I usually nudge the table and watch her face cringe as the water vibrates, making her point hard to prove. But this time nothing happens, as if the water's frozen, even though the glass isn't cold when I touch it.

My father, who's also at the table, peers over his morning paper and chuckles, like he's sharing a private joke with my mother. My sister, Irene, who's toying with her scrambled eggs while working on an extra-credit question for AP Biology, says, "Hmmmmmm." And my nine-year-old brother, Crash, angrily blurts out, "It's a dirty trick."

Normally, I pay as much attention to Crash as I do to the yelping of our pug dog, Spot, who's twelve years old, smells like a dead rat no matter how much we groom him, and has half his bottom teeth missing. But this time I say, "What's bugging you today, Crash?"

Crash has flaming-red hair and bright-green eyes the size of bottle caps. His skin's as pale as flour, but when he's mad, his face glows like a ripe tomato, and he's certainly mad now. He points angrily at my mother. "I heard her talking about it. She paid some guy to glue a piece of plastic in the glass. She got it made especially for you." Next, he's pointing at my father. "And *he* said to get it mounted like a trophy and have 'Benny Alvarez: Mr. Negativity' printed on it."

If Irene or I spoke like this to our parents, we'd be in lockdown for a week, but my mother leans over and pats Crash on the head, while my father lowers his newspaper, still amused.

"Don't call your mother 'she,'" he says.

"But it's a dirty trick."

Irene pauses from her extra-credit assignment, addressing Crash in the adult voice she uses when she's trying to act like a school counselor. "Crash," she says, "talk like that keeps you from being a productive human being." So Irene has finally realized Crash is an alien.

Now here's the hard part. Any other guy my age would tell his sister to stop acting superior, or he'd wait until later and mix some toothpaste into her acne cream. I've read all those books where the teenage older sister is nasty and moody and hates her brother, but Irene's the nicest person you'll ever meet. You could tell her a meteor is about to strike, and she'd be more interested in photographing it for posterity than running for cover.

"I'm already a human being," Crash says.

"And a cool one at that," Irene says, "but not very positive."

And there's truth to that. If I'm Mr. Negativity, Crash is the Cantankerous Kid, which is why everyone tiptoes around him, hoping he'll change and not set the house on fire, or maybe they feel bad for naming him Crash after a rich uncle who died on safari a hundred years ago.

But my sister still isn't done. "I think everyone in the family wants you to be happy, Crash, and as Mom says, it's all about attitude." With that, she looks around the table for support. For some reason, I nod (my sister can make you do things like that, like she's a good witch), my father laughs again, and my mother says, "We need to talk about school, Benny."

"School?"

"Yes, school."

My mother volunteers to help at recess, so she sees Ms. D almost every day, and in yesterday's "Benny discussion," my response to the science test came up.

"First, I must stress that Ms. Butterfield said you were not loud or disrespectful, but that your constant questions disrupted the exam."

"It depends on what you mean by 'constant questions.' If you need an answer, there's no limit to the number of questions you should ask."

My father lowers his paper, impressed by my reasoning.

"You're just trying to avoid responsibility for rude behavior, Benny," my mother says.

The Book would have said "weasel out," but I let it slide and go on. "You want me to get As in science, right?"

My father looks interested now, wondering where I'm going with this.

"Of course we do."

"Then how can I get an A if I don't understand the question?"

"He has a point, Margaret," my father says.

"Don't encourage him, Colin."

"I'm with Dad," Crash exclaims, the color of his face back to normal.

"You're all missing Mom's point," Irene interjects.

"Yes," my mother says, holding up the glass. "I had this made, hoping we'll avoid this conversation in the future. I thought you'd place it on your dresser, so it will be the first thing you see in the morning and you'll say, 'I'll go with the glass half full today.'"

Inspired by my mother's speech, Irene nods her head so vigorously, she almost falls off her chair.

Crash mumbles, "Fat chance."

And my father, trying to save face with my mother, says, "You never know, Benny," though he doesn't look too convinced.

"But first," my mother continues, "I need to know that you understand the symbolism of the glass."

"Come on, Mom," I say.

"So I don't have to repeat it?"

"Trust me, I get it."

So I take the glass upstairs and place it on my dresser. Why? First, because I made my point. Second, because I don't want to be late for school. And third, because I love my mother, and if she wants me to wake up every morning staring at this strange trophy, I'll do it, though I know I'll always see the glass as half empty. Irene, my mom, Ms. D, and I'm sure my archenemy, Claudine, would think that makes me negative, but that depends on how you define negativity.

THE BOOK

I was about seven when my mother first feared I was becoming "negative." It all started one morning after my father delivered one of his many rants on politics. My mother asked him to tone it down, saying the world wasn't going to end soon and that it was best to focus on all the good things people do. More important, she added, she was beginning to notice the same kind of attitude in me, as if she thought negativity was contagious, or passed down genetically, like blond hair and blue eyes.

"Negative?" my father protested. "I call it enthusiasm for my beliefs. Instead of plopping down in front of the TV, Margaret, I read and develop opinions. The rich are getting richer and want the rest of us to be their gardeners, and people might be more inclined to end these stupid wars if their own kids were soldiers. I don't like thinking about these things, but you can't just paste smiley faces on the refrigerator"—my mother does this—"or . . ." And as my father rampaged on, my mother looked at Irene, who was eleven at the time, both of them nodding knowingly at me and my father, as if to say "Case closed."

Later the word "negative" followed me around like a bad stink, and when a word seems tattooed on your forehead, when teachers, people you hardly know, call you something, it's time to examine the word.

Word Warriors to the rescue.

The Word Warriors are me and my best friends, Jocko and Beanie. Those aren't their real names, but they decided you needed a nickname to join our club. I don't blame them. Jocko's real name is Reginald and Beanie's is Jefferson. Beanie didn't like his name because he said no one trusts a kid with a last name for a first name, especially if he's black, and Jocko said he always wanted to be called Jocko after some WWF wrestler who died years ago in a car accident.

I told them I didn't want a nickname. I'm president of the club, so what could they say? I actually like my name, even though it doesn't fit. When people meet me, they expect me to speak Spanish because of the "Alvarez," but in fact, no one in my family looks Hispanic or speaks Spanish or has even been to Spain or South America or Mexico. I guess my father had a great-great-great-great-grandfather named Alvarez who married an Irishwoman. After that it was Irish plus Irish until my father married my mother, who's French. So if you're expecting a rush of Spanish when I get worked up, you're going to be disappointed.

Which brings me to the Book.

As I said, the Book is *Proteus: A Word Dictionary and Thesaurus for Children, with Explanations of Well-Known Phrases* by A. J. Logos. I came across it when Borders closed and they were having a huge book sale. At first, I refused to go with my father because he was bent on protesting the closing, wanting to give a tough time to "the buzzards feeding off the death of a beautiful animal." But I decided to give him moral support, and even he ended up buying a book on golf for my grandfather, though not until he had complained out loud for ten minutes to anyone who'd listen about "greedy corporations."

While he patrolled the store, I scanned the kids' section, coming across a pile of little blue books with gold emblems on the covers. Small enough to fit in your back pocket, they were stacked alongside hundreds of those stupid vampire novels Jocko reads. The dictionary part didn't blow me away, but when I paged through the thesaurus, I got excited. I guess I had always known about the thesaurus, but I had never held one in my hand. The first word I looked up was "dumb." I found "inarticulate, mute, silent, dim-witted, moronic, thick, dense," and the list went on. That's when I realized a thesaurus could actually be fun. For example, there's this one bully in school named Big Joe, and sometimes it's hard to tell whether he's a jerk or plain dumb, but I know if I call him dumb, he'll have three of his friends hold me down while he kicks soccer balls into my face. But I might be able to get away with "thick" or "dense," and if I call him "inarticulate," he'll think I'm complimenting him.

Now my mother would say I had discovered ammunition to aid me in my so-called negative approach to life, but, if you look at a thesaurus, even "negative" isn't the right word. Consider some of its synonyms: "adverse, antagonistic, contrary, dissenting, repugnant." You could see me as contrary or adverse, but that's not necessarily a bad thing. The Founding Fathers were contrary, and if they hadn't been, we'd all be talking funny and wearing bowler hats. And no one can ever accuse me of being repugnant. I wouldn't even like to be called antagonistic, but sometimes you have to be if you want to change something, and there's always something to change at school, especially with Claudine infecting the hallways with her nonsense.

Maybe none of this excites you, but Jocko and Beanie, after I gave them *Proteus*, could see the interesting possibilities of playing with words. Beanie nailed it after Jocko said one afternoon that he was "scared" of that week's English exam. Trying to cheer Jocko up, Beanie opened the Book and read, "'Scared: alarmed, dismayed, worried, terrified, paralyzed, upset.' No, Jocko, you aren't 'scared' of your exam. You're alarmed and worried and upset. You're scared of spiders, and terrified of your father, and paralyzed when you have to talk in front of class."

"Bravo!" I said.

"Thanks," Jocko said, "though I still feel scared."

In his own way, Jocko was right, but he still saw the logic of Beanie's comment, and he was the one who suggested we start a club. "Besides the thesaurus," he said, "let's use a new word or expression from the Book every day, but it's got to be a weird one, something the other two will have to guess at, and you can never know it's coming."

Beanie and I liked this idea. Then we all agreed to be what you might call an "exclusive" club, meaning we'd have only three members. If that sounds bad, then think of us as being "particular" or "classy," or if you want to be nasty, I guess we'll have to live with "narrow-minded" or "snobbish."

CRASH

This morning my father's driving me and Crash to school, and he's not too happy about it.

Normally, I walk Crash to his bus stop, then leave about fifteen minutes later, but we're having a bit of a crisis. I'm only about twenty yards away when he asks me to come back.

"I can't," I say, "or I'll be late."

"Benny Alvarez," he yells again, looking a bit freaked out, "come here right now." Sometimes Crash repeats things my mother says to me, which can be very annoying.

"Sorry, I can't."

We argue like this for a few minutes until some mom, who looks half asleep, says very sternly, "Benny, why don't

13

you help your brother?"

Since I can't exactly blow her off, I walk toward Crash, who's separated himself from his friends. "What the heck's going on?" I say.

"I wet my pants," he whispers.

"You what?"

He's got his backpack in front of his crotch, and now I understand why he didn't run after me.

"Look," I say, "I'll walk to the side of you, and let's both laugh like we're having a jolly old time, then we'll go home and change."

Crash looks suspiciously at me. "Is this a trick?"

"Jeez, Crash, I'm trying to help. I'm your older brother."

Once he realizes I'm not going to say "Hey, everyone, Crash just wet his pants. How weird is that?" he goes along with my plan. Halfway down the street, he says, "You won't tell Reggie and Jefferson, will you?"

"You mean Jocko and Beanie?"

"Just don't tell them or I'll run away."

"Run away?"

"I will. I swear."

"Why would I embarrass you like that?"

"Because you're a blabbermouth."

"The word is 'loquacious.'"

"A blabbermouth is a blabbermouth."

"You're one tough little dude," I say.

"Dad's going to kill me."

"Why will he kill you?"

"Because he always tells me to pee before I leave. He says, 'You don't want to be the kid who wets his pants on the bus,' and now I've done it."

"But you *didn't* wet your pants on the bus. You wet your pants at the bus stop." I'm trying not to laugh when I say this.

Crash looks at me suspiciously. "I'm dead meat," he says.

"Dad will handle it okay. He's just been upset about Grandpa." Which is true. In fact, we're all worried. My grandfather's eighty-five and coming off his second stroke. Although my father didn't have a great relationship with him as a kid, they've gotten closer over the years, and Crash and I try to hang with my grandfather whenever we can.

"I'm roadkill," Crash says.

"That's kind of dramatic."

"Not if you're the kid who wet his pants."

When we get to the house, my mother has left for work and Irene for school. My father peers up from his newspaper. He's about fifteen years older than my friends' dads, so he looks tired a lot. But he's in good shape, so most people think he's only about fifty. He has a receding hairline and

15

gold wire-rimmed glasses. Someone once said he looked "smart." I tracked down that word in the Book and think "professorial" works better. He actually was a high school history teacher, but now he's retired and works part-time at a local golf course's pro shop. Whenever someone asks why he retired early (at fifty-nine), he responds with three words: "Crash and Benny."

"I'm afraid to ask what this is about," he says matter-of-factly.

I have to give Crash credit because he gets right to the point. "I wet my pants. I know I'm a loser, so you don't have to say it."

In fact, my father has sometimes used the word "loser" when completely frustrated by us, but he's always spent the next two weeks apologizing for it, so I'm not sure why Crash is bringing it up.

"You're not a loser, Crash," my father says.

He points to his damp crotch. "Oh yes I am."

"Do you know why this happened?" my father asks.

"Why does it matter?" Crash says.

"It matters because you can't fix something if you don't know why it's broken."

This is an interesting conversation, but I wish he'd just let Crash change instead of lecturing him. I'm about five feet from Crash, and I can smell the urine. "I'm going to be late for school," I say.

"I'll drive you both."

"But I want to ride my bike."

"Right now, Benny, I don't care what you want."

Crash interrupts. "Can't you just tell me what the lesson is, so I can change?"

"The lesson is that you spent all morning complaining to your mother. You whined about the clothes she set out for you, you blamed her for misplacing your book, and you grumbled about your cereal being soggy."

"Well, it was."

"It got soggy while you were complaining."

I can't help smiling when he says this.

"What are you smiling about?"

"Nothing," I say.

My father turns back to Crash. "In short, you wet your pants because you spent the morning focusing on crap instead of taking care of business." He never would have said "crap" if my mother were here, and if he had a copy of the Book (which I once offered him), he could've chosen from "baloney, drivel, idiocy, hogwash, twaddle."

Crash responds by saying about twenty times in a row, "Okay, okay, okay," and then my father sends him upstairs.

Ten minutes later, we're on a brief stretch of the interstate because my father decides he wants a doughnut before taking us to school. He's dodging a black BMW that cuts us off. "Idiot," he says, making a hand gesture I've never seen before. It's like he wants to shoot the guy the finger but doesn't want to do it in front of us, so three fingers go up and flail in various directions before he slaps his hand down on the wheel. "These morons think they drive bumper cars."

"Mom doesn't like name-calling," Crash says.

"And I was actually going to buy you a doughnut, Crash," my father says.

"He's right, though," I add, even though you'd have to page through about a thousand synonyms for "moron" to do justice to Rhode Island drivers.

"And I was going to get you one too," my father says, obviously happy with himself.

Now, my mother would've seen this drama as a very "negative" way to start the day, and Irene, who hates conflict of any kind, would've had to be put on medication, but the three of us aren't too fazed by it. Just the opposite, because my father, in spite of his threat, ends up buying Crash and me apple fritters, then giving us high fives when he drops us off, as if the apple fritters were a reward for surviving each other or passing some kind of Alvarez test.

MS. DEMIGODDESS

In homeroom, Beanie says, "Where were you this morning? We waited for you at the bike rack."

"Long story," I say.

"Just the usual dementia praecox, I guess," Beanie says.

"A little early for wordplay, Beanie, don't you think?"

"You know the rules, Benny: there are no rules."

Big Joe, who's sitting in front of me, turns and says, "Geeks." Big Joe's head is the size of a basketball, but he has a tiny nose, like someone hit it with a hammer about a hundred times. He has a blond brush cut and dark-brown eyes. Just about every guy I know with blond hair has blue eyes, but it's like God was sleeping on the job when Big Joe was born. That would account for his huge arms, which inexplicably are attached to very tiny hands.

"Speaking of dementia praecox," Beanie says.

"If you write it down," Big Joe says, "I'll bet I could guess it."

"But then you'd be part of our club," Beanie says. "And *that* would be demented." He looks slyly at me, and Big Joe completely misses Beanie's word hint.

"Too easy now," I say. "Yeah, it was crazy at my house this morning. It was definitely dementia praecox."

"Not so fast. You got the dementia but not the prae-cox."

"That's not even English."

"No, it's Latin," a familiar, sarcastic voice butts in from behind. "It means 'premature.' So 'dementia praecox' means, put crassly, 'crazy before your time.'"

"How did you know that, Claudine?" Big Joe, some-what in awe, says. Big Joe is always gaping at Claudine. She could order him to kneel on his chair and bark like a puppy if she wanted to.

Claudine doesn't answer, but instead holds up a black book. It's a Latin dictionary she lugs around because she signed up for an experimental class. Some big-shot admin-istrator decided that we're all dummies unless we know Latin, so the school is offering a special section to sev-enth graders. After I discovered the Book, I almost signed

20

up, but my father said learning Latin is about as useful as speaking Martian.

Although Claudine annoys me, she's right that many English words come from Latin, so I always tell Beanie and Jocko not to play our game around her. I can't stand it when she acts superior.

"Anyone can look a word up," I say.

"You should know," she counters.

"Not true. We guess words from their contexts," I say, making myself feel smarter than I am.

Big Joe just won't stay out of it. "What's context?"

Context is something our English teacher Ms. Bogan taught us last year, but before I can answer, Beanie starts in. "It's like if I say, 'Big Joe is a constant vexation to his peers,' everyone knows Big Joe makes fun of everyone and threatens them, so it's easy to guess the meaning of the word 'vexation.'"

Big Joe squints, his left eyebrow jutting up about an inch higher than his right. He points his little index finger at Beanie. "Recess," he says.

Now Beanie's going to have to volunteer in the library if he doesn't want to get hassled, but he's smiling, so it must be worth it.

"You're just annoyed, Benny," Claudine says, "because I know more about words than you do."

21

"Yeah," Big Joe says, "what's your problem with Claudine?" Then he looks at her. "If he bugs you, let me know and I'll teach him a lesson."

"I don't have a problem with you," I say to Claudine. By now everyone in the class is listening.

Becky Walters starts fake-coughing into her hand, and Paige Burnett, another friend of Claudine's, says, "So not true."

"Well, I don't," I repeat.

"You can't even look at me when you talk to me," Claudine says.

She's right about that. Claudine has long, reddish-brown curly hair that falls over her shoulders. Her face is thin, her nose tiny, but she has big eyes that freak me out. They tend to sparkle every time she gets excited, which is always, sometimes morphing from green to blue for no apparent reason. All I know is that when she stares at me, I get very confused and feel my face redden. I've thought about mentioning it to Jocko because he's friends with a lot of girls, but he'd probably laugh at me.

Fortunately, before I can answer, Ms. D comes into the room, placing her satchel on her desk. She looks around, then at me, and says, "Have I interrupted anything, Benny?" as if she assumes I'm causing trouble. "No, Ms. Butterfield," I say. She's looking snazzy today in white

22

jeans, black sandals, and a red silk sleeveless top. She's also wearing a white pearl necklace. She has a round face and high cheekbones, her blue eyes seeming to have grown larger since she got her hair cut short. She looks like an older version of Claudine, especially because her hair is red. I mentioned that to Beanie once, and he said, "You're not going to start stalking her, are you?"

Jocko is the one who came up with Ms. Demigoddess. When we first saw her, Beanie said she was "hot," but that didn't work for Jocko, so he went to the Book. "Princess," "prima donna," and "goddess" didn't quite fit either, but "demigoddess" did, because a demigoddess is part human and part divine. I know that seems over the top, but then you haven't seen Ms. D. Even when she does simple things, like emptying her satchel, as she's doing now, she seems, well, I haven't found the right word for that yet.

She addresses the class. "As I told you, besides the usual spelling, writing, and grammar, we're going to focus on poetry for the month of October."

A major guy-groan follows.

"Why is it that boys hate poetry?" Ms. D says, waiting for a boy to answer, but Claudine beats us to it.

"Because they think they're supposed to," she says.

"Interesting," Ms. D says, placing her hands palms down on her desk and leaning forward. When she does

23

this, her necklace sways back and forth, kind of hypnotizing me.

"How about because it's dumb," Big Joe says, waiting for kids to laugh, but they don't, so he tries again. "I mean what good is poetry? No one talks it."

Paige Burnett, who's always writing stuff in her journal, then slamming it shut when you walk by, says, "People 'talk it' every day, you big goof."

"No name-calling," Ms. D says, though I can see she's more amused than angry.

You don't want to mess with Paige. She's smart and knows it. She wears these bright-purple glasses specked with silver, like she's proud of all the reading she does. She also plays lacrosse, and I get the feeling she could smack you around if you annoyed her. "What I mean," she says, composing herself, "is that poetry is music, like rap music"—then she gawks momentarily at Big Joe to emphasize his stupidity— "and we listen to it every day. Kids are always singing lyrics," and she goes on about how "poetry is also found in nature," followed by a lot of other strange ideas.

We can tell Ms. D is excited by this turn in the conversation because she's striding around on her long legs, making sweeping hand gestures. She gets so worked up about literature that she must be pretty pooped by the end of the day.

24

"Now we're onto something," she says. "Let's ask one of the Word Warriors what he thinks."

I'm hoping she's talking about Beanie, and I wish we had kept the club secret, but why have a club if you can't exclude people, and kids won't know they're excluded unless they know the club exists.

"What's your take on poetry, Benny?" she says.

My take is that I think less about poetry than I do about the two glands on Spot's rear end that the vet told us to massage twice a week.

I go for something simple. "It's not anything I really think about."

"But isn't the point of the thesaurus and synonyms to help us see the metaphorical implications of words, and isn't that what poetry is partly about?"

I can almost hear Claudine's head nodding crazily from behind.

"Huh?" is the best I can do.

Ms. D laughs. "Huh?"

"Sorry, Ms. Butterfield, but that's a little heavy for me." Now everyone's laughing, and Paige's face seems frozen between rage and pity for me.

Ms. D approaches my desk and places her hand on my shoulder. This is the first time she's ever touched me, and my heart is doing a strange kind of rumba.

"Not to worry, Benny," she says, then scans the entire class. "Even those of you who think you understand poetry and metaphor have a lot to learn, which is why my poet-friend Caulfield Thomas Jones is coming to class tomorrow."

"Not that dweeb," Beanie mumbles, but Ms. D pretends she doesn't hear him.

Caulfield Thomas Jones is a poet and novelist who's supposedly from England and who the school pays to make classroom visits, even though none of us have ever heard of his books.

"Now, let's get back to basics," she says. "I asked you to look up Jack London last night. What did you come up with, Paige?" For the next ten minutes, we all sit comatose, listening to how Paige stayed up until three a.m. making sure her paper would be longer than anyone else's.

GRANDPA

When I get home, my father's finishing up laundry. He seems distracted, so I know he's been working on his book about the stock market crash of 2008. I should say he's *rewriting* the book, because every time he sends it to a publisher, they tell him it's "too general."

"If I hear that one more time," he says, "I'm going to blow up something." You might think someone who talks like this is pretty crazy, but he exaggerates on purpose to jerk people around.

My mother would say this rant is a "negative response to rejection." But she's not saying anything right now, because she's at work. She's a hospital administrator. I'm not sure what she does, but that hospital must be the most positive one in Providence. I imagine nurses sticking smiley-face decals onto your head as they wheel you into the operating room.

"Where's Crash?" I ask, watching Dad empty the dryer.

"Up in his room."

"What for?"

"For shooting off his mouth."

"Boy, is he having a bad day."

"The whole world's having a bad day, Benny."

I let that one go. "Can I help?" I ask.

"With the world?"

"No, with the laundry."

"You don't think it's feminine to do housework?"

"Huh?"

"That's what Jocko or whatever-his-name-is-this-month said."

I try to place that conversation but can't.

"You were on the back porch talking about your English teacher again."

Now I recall Jocko saying something about my father being like a mom.

"You got Jocko wrong, Dad. He thinks it's cool you're home and that I have an older dad."

"He won't feel that way when I'm dead before you even

get to college. You know, three out of my five best friends have bitten the dust." He makes this point quite frequently, which annoys my mother, who's thirteen years younger than him. She thinks this kind of talk scares Crash, who has obviously demolished the mood of the house today. I often wonder whether he'd be different if my parents had called him Jay or Asher, since both those names mean "happy" in other languages.

"You'll live forever, Dad," I say.

He can always detect a fake positive response, so he ignores me. "Look," he says, "I'm going to finish this pile. Then we're taking your grandfather putting. He's not doing too well."

"You want me to get our clubs?" I say.

"Whatever you do, don't forget Crash's putter or we'll have to sedate him."

Ten minutes later, we're on the road to my grandfather's house in East Providence. It's a pretty uneventful ride. Crash seems exhausted by eight hours of his own orneriness, and my father doesn't discover any rich CEOs or incompetent drivers to yell at.

When we pull up to the house, my grandfather is sitting on the front porch, holding his putter between his legs. It's October but warm, so he's wearing tan shorts and a striped polo shirt, along with golf shoes and his blue

Navy PT Boat hat, whose headband is stained white with sweat. Strands of gray hair fall to his neck, and his arms and legs are spotted with different shades of brown moles, which my father says are the result of years of playing golf and being a mailman.

"Hi, Dad," my father says.

"Hi, Grandpa," Crash and I chime in. My grandfather's about the only person Crash seems happy around.

"That woman," my grandfather says, pointing behind him. His eyes, sky blue, seem agitated.

"That woman" is Gloria, my grandfather's second wife. He's been married to her for about thirty years, and all they do is fight.

"Two marriages," he says, "and I couldn't get it right. Boy, did you luck out with Marjorie." He has a little trouble standing, so my father helps him.

"It's Margaret, Dad."

"Yeah, whatever."

After the second stroke, my grandfather dodged paralysis, but he has trouble with names and can't make sense of words when he tries to read, which ticks him off. But he can still putt a ball around the practice green at Firefly, the par-three course where my father works.

"I'm going to whip you guys today," he says.

"If you can stand that long," Crash says.

Crash can get away with being a wise guy to my grandfather.

"What a mouth on that kid," my grandfather says, laughing. "A real Alvarez. What's his name again?" And then the words get jumbled up. "Cramp? Crap?"

"It's Crap, Grandpa," I say, my father scowling at me. And that's what he calls Crash for the rest of the day, with no one correcting him. Even Crash gives him a pass, knowing my grandfather's hearing a different word than the one coming out of his mouth.

"Well, let's get rolling," he says. "Let's get the show on the road. Let's kick some butt."

"Let's get you some socks first," my father says.

Crash and I look at my grandfather's feet, and sure enough, they're sockless. But he's not embarrassed, because he knows where to put the blame. "That woman," he says again, pointing toward the house.

My father ignores him, goes into the house, and returns with a pair of white ankle socks. Gloria's standing behind him, smiling. It's almost four thirty, but she's still in her bathrobe. A black hairnet holds the bulk of her gray hair in place. "Have fun," she says.

"Yeah, right," my grandfather says.

"You're the love of my life," she croons playfully, which makes us all laugh. Despite what my grandfather says, Gloria's okay, and she takes good care of him.

Before long, we're on the practice green at Firefly.

"One ball, one club," my grandfather says, holding up his putter. He brought the long one. The top of the shaft touches his chest, so he doesn't have to bend over, just sway it back and forth like a pendulum. We actually don't have a chance against him, because he practices on his living-room rug about two hours a day, putting balls into the mouth of a Dixie cup, which is pretty difficult.

Even if we could beat him, my father and I would lose on purpose, but not Crash. One day, my father got lucky and was a stroke ahead of my grandfather until he messed up the next two putts on purpose. When I mentioned it to him later, Crash said, "Grandpa wouldn't want to win that way. He's no weak Sally." A weak Sally is what Grandpa calls us when our putts come up short.

There are five holes on the practice green, and the idea is to play them twice, then add up our strokes. My grand-father decides how far away we should putt from by tossing a quarter behind his back. He gets really serious when he does this, like it's a ritual handed down from Alvarez to Alvarez since the beginning of Alvarez time.

Crash, with his little putter, almost beats him today, but his last putt goes four feet past the hole. He uninten-tionally lets slip a swear word, and my father says, "Totally unnecessary, Crash." But then my grandfather's putt ends up short, and he says the same word, waddling over to Crash and placing his brown-spotted hand on Crash's shoulder. "Never up, never in," he says, and Crash nods, smiling broadly. My father just shakes his head, and for a moment, I'm a little jealous of Crash, wanting my grandfather all to myself.

After golf, we go to McDonald's, and my grandfather abuses the counter people because they won't let him use his senior discount to pay for everyone's meal. He does this every week, so they're used to it. Then we take him home. Gloria's waiting at the front door in the same outfit, ready for round fifteen. She invites us in, but my father says my mother's expecting us for dinner.

On the way home, I apologize to Crash for letting the "Crap" thing go on. "You know Grandpa would've beaten up on himself if he knew he messed up your name."

"Well, you could've gone with Cramp."

"Yeah, I guess so," I admit.

"Is he losing it?" Crash asked.

"Strokes aren't like that," my father says. "They mess up your wiring, so he has to try to retrain his brain, like he did the last time. Now even reading's been taken away from him."

"Who took it away?" Crash asks.

"Fate," I say. I'm not sure where that comes from, but my father seems to agree with me, while Crash probes the inside of his cheek with his tongue and nods, repeating his favorite phrase, "It's a dirty trick."

"It is what it is," my father says.

MOVING TARGETS

It isn't unusual for my father to become more serious when talking about my grandfather. From what I've heard over the years, they butted heads most of their lives, and I guess my grandfather was pretty hard on him, especially when he was a teenager, which is hard to believe, considering how laid-back and jokey he is with me and Crash. Sometimes when the four of us are together, it's like we're all fighting for my grandfather's attention: my father probably trying to make up for those lost teenage years, and Crash and me jockeying to be top grandson. When we were much younger, at a birthday party for my grandfather, I remember us pushing and shoving to see who'd help him blow out the candles, my grandfather seeming to enjoy it all.

One day, shortly before his first stroke, he and I were hitting golf balls off a green mat into a stretch of black netting he had tacked across the back of his garage, and I surprised myself by asking if he liked Crash more than me. He moved the mat a few feet onto the driveway, so we wouldn't break a club on our upswings; then he teed up an old range ball. *Whack!* I heard, the ball's flight cut short by the net. He leaned on his driver with one hand and rubbed his chin with the other, saying, "What makes you think I like Crash better than you?"

"Maybe 'better' isn't the right word, but you always cut him slack."

"Crash acts like a tough guy," he said, "but he's a gentle soul. That kind of Alvarez is born with a 'Handle with Care' sign around his neck."

I laughed. "Crash, a gentle soul?"

He teed up another ball and swung hard. *Whack!* "Your father was like Crash, Benny, and I made some mistakes there."

"I've heard."

He seemed taken aback by this confession. "Come here a second," he said, placing another ball on the mat. "Let me see you swing."

I grabbed a five iron and made a pass at the ball, following its low trajectory into the net.

"Take a shorter backswing," he said. "That shot would've never made it over the water hole at Firefly."

He was trying to distract me, but I wouldn't let him off the hook. "Are you proud of me, Grandpa?" I said.

He sighed deeply, then brushed some hair away from my eyes, as if admiring me. "Every day, Benny. You're our Golden Boy."

"Golden Boy?"

He laughed, stepping away a few feet. "Oh, you're a pain-in-the-neck Alvarez, all right, but you have your mother's grit and heart."

"That's not what I hear from everyone else."

"Then you'll have to prove them wrong. But I trust my instincts. Just be yourself, Benny. The real trick is to be crafty, kind of like a boxer, learning when to punch and when to duck and dodge. As my father once said, 'Trouble can't hit a moving target.'"

"Trouble, Grandpa?"

He didn't answer but instead asked for my five iron. "You need a stronger grip," he said, positioning his hands around the top of the club's shaft to demonstrate. "See what I mean?"

I grabbed the club and followed his suggestion, happy to see the ball take flight toward the top of the net.

ALDO

My sister's looking nervous this morning. Aldo's picking her up for school, and he's not one of my father's favorite people. I think he wanted her first real boyfriend to be a clean-cut jock with a social conscience, but Aldo's got long, stringy black hair and looks like an undertaker: black jeans, black Converse low basketball shoes, a black T-shirt with the name of some rock group on front, and a black jean jacket. I read somewhere that Albert Einstein had seven of the same outfits hanging in his closet, one for every day of the week, so he could focus on the meaning of the universe instead of worrying if the green tie went with the brown sports coat. Likewise, I imagine Aldo's closet being a sea of black denim.

What really drives my father bonkers, though, is that Aldo has a yellow tattoo of Tweety Bird on his neck. My father would've hated any tattoo, but Tweety Bird? What the heck is that about? We're almost afraid to ask.

Surprisingly, Aldo's a good basketball player; actually, a great basketball player. He often shoots hoops with me, even though I make a point to frequently bust him because his cockiness rubs me the wrong way. Once, when I asked him why he didn't play for the school team, he proudly said, "Team sports suck. Coaches suck. Been there, done that." The next time I saw him I said, "Did you mean 'suck' as in 'stinks' or 'rots'?"

He smiled broadly, though it wasn't a friendly smile, more like one of those I'm-about-to-smack-your-punk-behind smiles. "I meant sucks as in sucks," he said.

Ironically, Aldo's cockiness is the only reason my father tolerates him. Anyone who goes against the status quo is okay with him. But he still can't get past the tattoo. Also, the fact that Aldo is a drummer and lead vocalist in a band named the Cro-Magnons. You would've thought a guy who has a tattoo of Tweety Bird on his neck would've called his band the Flintstones, but Aldo told my parents they were looking for "something prehistoric, something primeval." At the word "primeval," my father's eyeballs widened about a quarter of an inch, and even my mother flinched. It was downhill for Aldo after that. If he had said "archaic" or "antediluvian" instead of "primeval," my parents wouldn't have been so terrified for dear sweet Irene. But none of it mattered, anyway, because Aldo could've been a budding serial murderer and Irene would have turned him to the good side.

I'm actually feeling sorry for her today, as she's sitting nervously, waiting for Aldo to show. We have a wide-open kitchen attached to the family room. Irene's at the kitchen table, checking her watch, pretending to flip through the pages of a novel. My mother's emptying the dishwasher, and my father's on his leather recliner, reading the paper, so he can have a ringside seat when Aldo arrives. Crash is upstairs for hiding the TV's remote because my mother wouldn't let him watch a rerun of *Good Luck Charlie*.

When the doorbell rings, everyone freezes except for me and Spot, who's barking and attacking the screen door. I open it a crack, and Aldo says, "Is Irene home?"

"No," I say. "She ran off with a Russian ballet dancer."

"I thought it was a Bulgarian prince."

"That was last week."

Aldo smirks. "Well, tell her I'll have the car running."

"I'm telling the truth this time," I say.

He starts to walk to his car, an old black BMW with a sharp-toothed caveman painted on the hood. I have to

40

admit, it's pretty cool. Suddenly, he turns and says, "Tell your father I miss him."

Before I can reply, Irene's at the door with her backpack. "You're impossible," she says, kissing me on the cheek, "but I love you." Sometimes I wish she'd smack me or cut holes in the crotch of my jockey shorts.

I watch her get into Aldo's car and drive away, thinking his car and Irene's personality are oddly contradictory. To my father, it's probably like watching Alice in Wonderland disappear on Attila the Hun's horse. I sit down on the couch and look up "contradictory": "inconsistent, incompatible, supine" (forget that one), and finally come to what I'm looking for, "incongruous." "Aldo and Irene are an incongruous couple." That's my phrase for Beanie and Jocko today.

"Is it really necessary to tease Aldo?" my mother asks.

"All great heroes have to pass a test," I say, echoing one of my father's expressions.

She looks professional today in a light-blue pants suit. She has long, curly blond hair and green eyes. I wish I had gotten that hair. Mine is straight and black, so I keep it short. My father says I got the Black Irish gene, whatever that means.

"I find this constant teasing negative and a waste of time," she says.

There's that word again.

"You can also see it as humorous," my father interrupts.

"What could possibly be funny about telling that poor boy every morning that Irene has eloped with assorted strange men?"

"*Repetition* is a fundamental staple of comedy," my father says. "We laugh at comedians when they keep hitting themselves in the face with a hammer. That's why Charlie Chaplin was so famous."

"I'm not one of your students, Colin," she says, then turns her attention to me. "Anything unusual happening in school today?" She says it as if she already knows.

"No," I say.

"Not even in Ms. Butterfield's class?"

"Not that I know of."

"Not something to do with poetry?"

"Oh yeah," I say, as if just remembering, then add, "What do you do, talk to her every day?"

"It was on the website."

"Really?"

"Yes, it's always exciting when a guest visits. Ms. Butterfield has brought that dimension to your school."

I'm about to respond, impressed by her use of "dimension," but Crash interrupts from upstairs. "I'm going to be late for my bus," he says. He's right, so I walk him there,

42

returning just in time to meet up with Beanie and Jocko, who are parked by my front door on their bikes.

"Aldo and Irene are an incongruous couple," I say.

"Wow, you're on your game today," Jocko says. He's a big kid with a round face, a buzz cut, and so many freckles his face glows like a wet pumpkin. His size makes him appear tough, but he's no bully. In fact, he can be kind of nervous and is a compulsive worrier. Most girls I know worry, so maybe that's why they like him.

"You don't have to answer now," I say.

"I can't even tie my shoes this early," Beanie says.

Jocko seconds that, so we hop on our bikes and head to school.

MR. CONGO

At first, this morning seems free from drama, except for a couple of warnings from the principal, one about wearing baseball hats in school because they're associated with gangs. About the only gang you'll find in my middle-class neighborhood is a posse of paunchy new moms gathering every morning on the school track to chat and trot behind baby joggers.

After that announcement I'm off to Mr. Congo's (that's his real name) math class, where we've been playing Crunching Numbers for the last two weeks. It supposedly helps us to review concepts for the inane state exams given every fall. The kids hate them, the teachers hate them, and my father, who reads more about the demise of our public school system than the secretary of education, hates them, but obviously, some screwball in Washington decided they make us smarter. The Crunching Numbers period usually ends up being a battle between the boys and girls, a battle we actually win sometimes, much to the annoyance of Claudine and her gang.

This morning, Mr. Congo looks like he wrestled three pit bulls on the way to class. He's only in his twenties, but he's bald and has dark circles under his eyes. Add to the bald head and baggy eyes that he's thin and pale, and you could easily mistake him for a convict just released from solitary. To be fair, Mr. Congo's wife had a baby a month ago, and it's clear he's not sleeping much. If Claudine didn't water all the strange, cool plants his wife arranged in the classroom the first day of school, they wouldn't have lasted a week.

But Claudine's not too happy this morning. Five minutes left to go in class and the final Crunching Numbers question lights up the screen: $(5x + 2x) = (4x - 3y)$ "Tick, tick, tick," I say, realizing she and her gang don't have a clue. "Tick, tick, tick," I say, rubbing it in before tapping the little bell on my desk and giving the correct answer.

"You the man," Beanie yells, and before Mr. Congo can lecture us about being "gracious" (a favorite word of his), we're off to English class.

Claudine's ahead of me in the hall, so I slow down,

not wanting to invade her unhappy space, but I know she feels my nearness because I swear she's slowing down on purpose. The more slowly she walks, the more I try to lag behind until we're crawling toward Ms. D's room.

Suddenly, I'm pushed from behind. "Get moving, Alvarez." It's Big Joe. "What are you, crippled?"

Before I can respond, I find myself careening into Claudine.

She wheels around, obviously as uncomfortable with this encounter as I am, and Paige, who's walking beside her, glares at me like I'm a laboratory rat she's about to dissect on a black slab she has concealed in her basement.

I can feel the blood vessels swelling in my face, and I'm trying to calm down, but it's harder than getting rid of the hiccups.

"Big Joe pushed me," I say, my victory in math class a distant memory.

"No, I didn't," Big Joe lies.

"Yes, you did," Beanie chimes in.

Claudine suddenly seems taller and older and speaks in that voice Irene uses when trying to convert me or Crash to her cult of positivity. She places one hand on her hip and says, "Your excuses don't matter much, Benny, but an apology does."

"Well, *I* think his excuse matters," Beanie says.

46

"Forget it, Beanie," I say, knowing it's too late. Claudine has turned the tables, my brief advantage destroyed by a simple push.

"Well?" she says, expressionless.

I don't know why I wimp out so easily, but I say, "Sorry."

I'm waiting for her to accept or not accept it, or kick me in the shins, but she turns and strolls into Ms. D's class.

"What just happened?" I ask Beanie.

Big Joe laughs. "You got punked, dude."

I look to Beanie for support, but he seems seriously disappointed. "When it comes to that girl, dude, you have to toughen up."

The last thing I hear before walking into Ms. D's room is Big Joe's stupid laugh.

CAULFIELD THOMAS JONES

Ms. D's room looks different today. There are twenty kids in class, and normally groups of four desks are arranged in five separate squares, so we're forced to face one another while Ms. D roams the room. Some guys don't like this setup. They're usually the ones who nod off, and that's hard to do when you're staring across at another student, who's always a girl. Ms. D makes sure of that. I sit with Beanie and Clare Davis and Bethany Briggs. I don't have a problem with those girls because they're what I call neutrals: girls who don't pile on when Claudine goes after me or one of the other guys.

But as I said, things are very different today. Actually, two things. First, the desks are rearranged, so two desks are side by side. Second, Caulfield Thomas Jones is sitting on Ms. D's desk with his feet on her chair, his arms crossed, like the classroom is a beach and he's the head lifeguard.

Ms. D is making everyone line up along the chalkboard. "We're doing something very different today," she says.

No kidding.

"And we have a special guest," she adds, pointing to Caulfield Thomas Jones (from here on known as Caulfield). "Mr. Jones has come to talk about poetry and challenge us to participate in a friendly competitive exercise."

Caulfield's about six feet tall with short, curly brown hair and blue eyes, and he's more hyper than Crash after four Reese's Cups. It doesn't look like he's faking his love of literature, so you have to give him some credit, though Beanie's leery of him because he thinks Caulfield's English accent isn't real, and because, according to Beanie, "The only thing worse than having a last name for a first name is having a last name for a first name and two more to boot."

But Ms. D loves this guy, and they tend to make private jokes, then look goofy at each other.

The last time he visited, he laid out all these different things on the floor—a world map, a page from the sports section, an empty coffee cup from McDonald's, some toy soldiers—and we were supposed to place them in a short story. That really threw Big Joe, but I liked it.

I can't say I feel the same way about poetry. In fact, I'd rather have Big Joe give me a wedgie than listen to Caulfield Thomas Jones recite Shakespeare or whatever he's planning today.

"This exercise," Ms. D says, "will involve boys and girls working together in pairs."

A collective groan goes up from the class, and Ms. D looks to Caulfield for support.

"It's not as if you're second or third graders," he says, then addresses the boys, adding, "Girls are people too," which makes Ms. D laugh louder than I've ever heard her laugh before.

Old Caulfield obviously has some weird ideas on how we feel about girls. We're not afraid of them, and I don't dislike Claudine or Paige because they're girls but because they're troublemakers. Which is why I'm nervous about being paired with one of them. I'm trying to decide which one would be my worst nightmare when Ms. D announces the first two victims.

"We'll start with Benny," she says, scanning a list of names on her desk, turning toward Caulfield, and saying, "Benny is the wordsmith I mentioned to you." I make a mental note to look up "wordsmith" in *Proteus*, while she says, "And Benny will be working with . . . Sara Samuels."

Man, did I luck out. Sara is a neutral, a shy, quiet girl. She's the smartest kid in English class and has always had a crush on me, so I'm thinking she'll go along with what I say.

Ms. D announces the rest of the names and we take our seats very quickly, so that Caulfield will have a half hour to do his thing. The only weird pairing is Big Joe and Paige, which gets a loud laugh from the class, since it's like putting Shrek and Selena Gomez together.

Caulfield begins with some exercises on metaphor, writing on the board, "My love is a red rose" and "My love is like a red rose," asking which one is a metaphor, which a simile. That's easy and boring, but then things get interesting when he says, "How can your beloved, or love in general, be a red rose? Isn't a red rose a red rose?"

Claudine pounces on that one. "It's really a red rose," she says, "but has things in common with love."

"Can you explain that more clearly, young lady?" Caulfield says.

Claudine's thinking hard, but it's clear she doesn't have a quick answer. I'm waiting, actually hoping, for her to blush, but I guess it's not in her makeup.

Caulfield gives her a bit longer, then says, "Why don't we ask the wordsmith?" I'm looking around the classroom, wondering who he's talking about, until I remember it's

51

me. He points to the sentences again, leaping off Ms. D's desk like he just sat on a wasp. "Let's start with the literal things we associate with a rose."

I think about this, then say, "A rose grows, it's beautiful, it kind of glows in the sun."

Caulfield's really worked up now, writing each of my responses on the board, then asking the class what they have to do with love, and everyone begins to see the connections. "Love grows too," Paige says.

"And it's beautiful," Sara adds, looking a little too longingly at me.

"And sometimes people blush when they're in love," Beanie says, not knowing he'll take a pounding for that one later.

"But it also has thorns," I say.

"Mr. Happiness to the rescue," Claudine says, shaking her head disgustedly.

"But Benny's right," Caulfield responds, and I'm thinking, *You go, Caulfield,* surprised to discover this unlikely ally.

"What does love have to do with a thorny rose, Benny?"

"It can hurt," I say.

"And that's what makes this metaphor so powerful."

I'm waiting for the class to lift me onto their shoulders and carry me to the cafeteria, where I'll be fed a giant

52

banana split, but no one but Caulfield seems overly excited, so he offers a few more metaphors, then moves to what he calls object poems, one cool one called "Hanger":

> Hanger
> Protean instrument,
> I bow curved-neck before you.
> Yes, you are a child's toy:
> a metal bow for straw arrows,
> a back scratcher, a toothless smile,
> you old extended question mark, you,
> I offer you in amazement
> the shirt off my back.

He explains that like Proteus, the shape-shifting Greek god, a hanger, too, resembles many different objects and has many different purposes, and that the poet thinks this is so cool that he bows "curved-neck" to the hanger. "It's a simple poem," he says, "but after reading it, you'll never look at a hanger the same way again."

Finally, Caulfield gets to our assignment. We're supposed to work with our partner to write a short object poem but not divulge the title, so he and the class can guess it at a later date. He also says he'll give out a few prizes for the best poems. "You don't have to write verse or rhymed poems," he says. "You can write prose poems or even sentences," and he gives us a few examples: "Snow that falls on a tree stump but doesn't melt" (gray hair), "A black string in one's path" (ants), and also a few poems written in short paragraphs.

Claudine isn't very happy about Caulfield's suggestions. "How can poetry be poetry if it doesn't rhyme or have line breaks?" she says.

Caulfield smiles. "Isn't poetry elevated language and interesting comparisons? Why can't you have that in a sentence or paragraph?" Then he reads a description of a rainstorm from a novel, and it certainly sounds like poetry.

"Well, *we're* not going to do that," Paige says, staring down Big Joe, making it clear who's going to run that group.

Ms. D, sensing the period is about to end, wraps things up by saying, "With the time remaining today, why don't you brainstorm with your partner and choose an object you both feel is suitable. As Caulfield says, an object can be an animal or an emotion, or most anything." Then she and Caulfield mosey off to a corner of the room and chat.

When Sara and I finally get down to business, she looks very concerned. "We're not going to write one of those prose poems, are we, Benny?" I actually had assumed we were, stupidly forgetting that Sara probably takes poetry very seriously, first of all because she's a girl, and second because, like Paige, she's always scribbling something down in a journal. With my luck, it's probably rhyming poetry.

"Why don't we deal with that later?" I say.

She doesn't seem too enthusiastic but agrees. After going through a number of possibilities, we decide on a worm, thinking if we can turn that into poetry, we'll knock their socks off. That choice was really Sara's, but then I suggest a night crawler, those worms my grandfather and I catch at night before we go fishing. When it's time to leave, Ms. D seems very pleased with the class, and at recess, Beanie and I tell Jocko about the assignment.

"Boy, I'm glad I'm not in her class," Jocko says.

"It was actually pretty cool the way Caulfield described it," I say.

"Caulfield? I thought you hated the guy."

"I never said that."

"You should listen to yourself sometimes."

"Whatever, he was okay today."

"He really was, Jocko," Beanie adds.

Jocko starts laughing, then looks at me and says, "Incongruous."

"What?"

"Irene and Aldo are an 'incongruous couple' because they don't fit. It's like a banana going out with an apple."

"Very good, Jocko," I say, thinking about Big Joe and Paige.

"Yeah," Beanie says, "maybe *you* should write our poems, Jocko."

"No thanks, I'm uptight enough about what to get Becky Walters for a birthday gift."

"Birthday?" Beanie says.

"Yeah, her party's next Saturday afternoon. You mean you guys weren't invited?"

"Since when are girls inviting guys to their birthday parties?" I ask.

"Well, it's happening now. She's having a deejay and everything."

"Like dancing?" I ask, my legs suddenly going numb.

"I guess, but I'm not going without you guys. I'll tell Becky that."

"Don't worry about it," I say, knowing this is a party I don't mind missing.

"Well, I'm going to check into it tomorrow."

"When did you get your invitation?" Beanie asks.

"Yesterday."

"Let's hope ours got lost in the mail," Beanie says to me.

"You guys are really weird when it comes to girls," Jocko says.

I don't think that's true. To be "weird when it comes to girls," you have to think about them a lot, and that's not something I do.

"YOU GOTTA LOVE THIS KID"

After school, I shoot hoops with Jocko, so I don't get home until about five. My father isn't around, and I'm surprised to see Crash and my grandfather sitting side by side on the steps of our large back porch. Crash is brandishing a huge Nerf gun, which looks like one of those old Gatling machine guns. He's aiming it at the bird feeders, which are hanging on cast-iron poles at opposite ends of our koi pond. The gun holds about twelve Nerf bullets, which, contrary to the manufacturer's claim, can put a dent in your cheek. It's a quiet, sunny afternoon, the little birdies chirping and the koi pond's artificial waterfall babbling, so I'm wondering what poor creature Crash plans to annihilate, and how he enlisted my grandfather in this attack.

"What's going on?" I ask.

Crash turns and angrily whispers, "Shhh, you'll scare it away." It's obvious he's been crying, because his cheeks are stained with dried tears.

I lower my voice. "It?"

"The hawk," Crash says.

My grandfather tells me to go inside, where he'll explain. "You okay by yourself?" he says to Crash, and Crash nods. "If that bum shows up, give 'im both barrels, you hear?"

It takes me a while to get my grandfather into the kitchen, where we sit on bar stools at a tall round granite table facing a window that looks out onto the backyard.

"What happened, Grandpa?"

Nowadays, it's not always easy to get a straight answer from my grandfather, but after I help him find the right words, events come into focus. As it turns out, when Crash came home, he sat outside with my grandfather, doing his homework. As moody as Crash is, he has a few places he finds peaceful, like the porch. He loves birds, so he's in charge of filling the bird feeders, and he keeps track of species that stop by. He's even researched the kinds of seeds that attract different birds.

But as he was sitting there today, a large hawk swooped

down, grasped a robin in its claws, then soared away. It's probably the hawk we've seen hanging around on lower branches the last few weeks. I thought its presence was odd, though cool, because I had never seen one up close.

"How did you know about this?" I ask my grandfather.

"Your father called, and . . ." He's trying to grab hold of Crash's name among the jumble of choices whanging around in his head.

"Crash, Grandpa."

"Yeah, Crash said you're all a bunch of losers and he just wanted me here."

I almost laugh, imagining my father's response to that.

"If Crash doesn't want the hawk to attack the birds, why did he tell me not to scare it away?"

"Revenge," my grandfather says.

"So where's Dad?"

"He went grocery shopping. Some other guy's on his way." And he begins searching for a name again. "Dodo or Bilbo, something like that."

"Aldo?"

"Yeah, that's it. Sounds like a dog, doesn't it?"

"Why's he coming?"

"Don't know," my grandfather says.

After I get him a glass of water, we return to the back porch, sitting on opposite sides of Crash.

"Sorry," I say. "It must have been pretty traumatic."

He looks straight ahead. "Why would you care? You think hawks are cool."

"Not this one, Crash. He's a bad apple."

He looks up at me. "You mean that?"

"Yeah, he's one nasty hawk."

"You think this gun will scare him away?"

"If it doesn't, we'll get a bigger gun, right, Grandpa?"

"You bet. One of those flamethrowers will do the trick."

"But wouldn't it fry the bird feeders?" Crash says.

"Then we'll have to buy them special suits. What are they, Benny?" he asks.

"Asbestos suits, Grandpa?"

"Yeah, those."

This makes Crash smile.

"Why's Aldo coming over, Crash?" I ask.

"When I got upset, I called Irene, and Aldo said the same thing happened to him once, so he knows what to do."

"Hmmm," I say.

"Will you do me a favor?" Crash asks.

"Sure."

"Hold the gun while I go inside and pee."

"No problem," I say, taking the weapon from him.

"You'll pay attention, right? You won't start talking

to Grandpa and space out, will you?'

"Why would I do that?"

"Because you're a blabbermouth."

Grandpa lets out a loud laugh, saying, "You gotta love this kid."

ALDO AUDUBON

When my father comes home, I'm surprised my mother's with him.

"Crash called you, too?"

"No, I ran into your father at the grocery store."

"Very romantic," I say, and she smirks at me. Irene, my grandfather, and I are sitting at the granite table, drinking Cokes. Aldo's outside with Crash, moving the bird feeders around. He's being very scientific, spreading the branches of our small trees, gesturing to Crash, who's holding a bird feeder in each hand.

"What's the Missing Link doing here?" my father asks.

"That's not funny," Irene says.

"Really," my mother adds.

My grandfather laughs and says, "He's a real kook, heh? But if Crap likes him, he's okay with me. But what's with the tight black pants? And the kid's got no behind."

My mother says, "It's Crash, Kieran." (Kieran is my grandfather's name.)

"That's what I said."

My father places a bag of groceries on the kitchen counter and says to my mother, "I'll explain later."

Irene comes quickly to Aldo's defense. "I know you think Aldo eats raw meat and beheads people, but he knows a lot about animals and flowers."

"Is he gay?" my grandfather asks.

"Kieran," my mother says, and I add, "Very uncool, Grandpa."

Meanwhile Aldo and Crash come in for a glass of water, and my mother says that won't do, so she tells me to grab some Powerades from a refrigerator we keep in the garage.

"Not necessary, Mrs. Alvarez," Aldo says, but she insists. Then she hugs Crash. "I'm really sorry, Buddy. You want some popcorn?"

The trouble with "positive" people is they think everything has a simple solution. Right now, Crash wants to suffer. He wants to cry, then track down that hawk and Nerf-dart it to death.

"Did you hear me, Benny?" she asks, and so I leave.

When I return, Aldo is sitting in my seat next to my grandfather, while my sister edges her chair next to his and starts rubbing his forearm. My father takes this in but doesn't seem upset.

"So what's the verdict, Aldo?" he says.

"If we move the bird feeders closer to the trees," Crash jumps in, "Aldo says the birds will be able to hide from the hawk or escape easier."

"But then the squirrels will eat their food," I say.

Aldo nods. "But you can still keep the feeders away from the squirrels but close enough to give the birds protection. We're going to fiddle with them and see what happens."

"So a few more birds may have to bite the dust?"

"Benny," my mother says.

"I'm just saying, that's the only way we'll know."

Grandpa's feeling a little upstaged, so he offers his two cents. "Not if Crap and me are on patrol, and there's always the flamethrowers."

Aldo's looking like he just entered an alternate universe. He mouths silently to Irene, "Crap?" and then he speaks in a normal voice to my grandfather, "Flamethrowers?"

But Crash has changed his mind about the flamethrowers. "No, Grandpa. Aldo explained it's not the hawk's fault. They have to live too, and without birds, they'll die."

"Really?" my grandfather says, looking impressed.

"But Aldo says the hawk will come back, so we can at least try to protect the little birds."

"So no flamethrowers or automatic weapons?" my grandfather says. "How about a bazooka?"

"No," Crash says.

"Too bad—it would've been fun."

My father and Aldo laugh loudly at this comment, then look surprised and uncomfortable by their sudden camaraderie, and my father stuns everyone, except Irene, by inviting Aldo to dinner.

"Me too?" Grandpa says.

"Of course, Dad."

Aldo and Crash leave to finish their bird feeder relocation job, and the rest of us set the table, while my father thaws out hamburger for tacos. My grandfather stays put, and I see him watching Crash and Aldo. At one point, he grabs my arm and says, "You think he's a kook?"

"What?"

"The guy with the tight pants."

"No, Grandpa, he's not a kook."

"Then what is he?" Grandpa asks.

"He's a good guy, just a little different."

I look up and notice my father's been listening. He's rubbing his chin between his thumb and forefinger, like he's wondering how he would've answered Grandpa's question.

Later, for the heck of it, I look up "kook": "blockhead, bonehead, dork, imbecile, jerk, nitwit, out to lunch." The jerks at Aldo's school probably call him a dork, or think he's out to lunch, but I'm beginning to think he's what you'd call an original, since I never met anyone quite like him.

Still, there's that Tweety Bird tattoo.

A DOG NAMED HOBO

Jocko, Beanie, and I get to school early the next morning, so we rack our bikes and sit on the front lawn. It's cool but sunny. We watch kids shuffling toward us, envying the eighth graders, who get to leave next year for what Beanie calls the "real world," high school. We're about to grab our backpacks when I spy Claudine walking toward the entrance with her old tan Labrador retriever, Hobo. Everyone knows about the dog, how he's the oldest dog in the universe and has some weird cancer but just won't die. He walks Claudine to school every morning, then shows up right on time for dismissal.

"You have to admit that's cool," Jocko says.

"What?" Beanie asks.

"The way that dog waits for her every day."

"I thought the town had leash laws," I say.

"What, do you want to throw a half-blind dog with cancer in the pound?"

"I'm just saying that if it were Spot, they wouldn't let *me* do it."

"And they'd be right," Jocko says, "because that dog smells like a garbage dump."

"I just think Claudine gets treated differently because her mother's a teacher." She's actually an aide.

"I agree," Jocko says, "so why don't we go over and beat old Hobo with some sharp sticks."

Beanie laughs.

"I'm not saying that."

"Dude, you're just very harsh on that girl."

I'm wondering why everyone keeps saying that.

"Speaking of Claudine, who happens to be a girl," Beanie says, "has everyone gotten their behest?"

It takes me and Jocko about two minutes to figure out he's talking about the invitation to Becky Walters's party.

"Yeah," I say, "yesterday. But no reason to worry about presents. Mine said to donate money to the breast cancer crusade."

"Breast cancer?" Jocko says. "How did I miss that? You think her mother has it?"

I hadn't really thought about that. "I don't know."

"Are you going?" Beanie asks me.

Last night, after Aldo left, I really sweated that one. In a way, it's not something I want to miss, because I've never been to a party with a deejay. So many unknowns, it's almost interesting, but I'm having trouble getting past the idea of dancing. Irene says the girls will dance with or without us, and she'll be happy to teach me a few steps. What no one knows is that I dance by myself sometimes, doing what comes naturally, though the thought of dancing publicly makes me want to puke.

"I asked if you're going," Beanie repeats.

"Yeah," I say, "but only if we show up together. I don't want to be there early with a bunch of girls or guys I don't even like."

"I agree," Jocko says. Then he starts obsessing on a lot of little details, like how we should dress and if we should wear something pink because of the breast cancer thing.

It's amazing how he'll freak over every dumb detail of everything we do but spaces out on the big stuff, like the fact that girls will be at the party. But then, as I said, he'll talk to a girl as easily as he'll talk to a guy.

Once we agree we're going, we head toward the entrance. Hobo's lying at Claudine's feet while she talks to a friend. "Let's wait a second," I say.

Beanie agrees, but Jocko ignores us, moving toward the front doors. He's almost there when he takes a detour to pet Hobo, who's resting on his side. Jocko rubs his belly and Hobo's left leg starts twitching. Now here's the weird part: while he's rubbing Hobo, he's talking to Claudine like they're old friends.

"What's that about?" I say.

"You know Jocko," Beanie says.

As Jocko continues to talk, my feet lead me involuntarily toward Claudine, and before I know it, I'm next to her, then on one knee petting Hobo. I look behind to see if Irene is there, zapping me with a do-gooder spell.

"Nice dog," I say, waiting for Jocko to add, "Yeah, why don't we call a vet to put him down?" but he gives me a pass.

Claudine's towering over me, squinting, probably wondering if this is some kind of trick. She doesn't thank me, just helps Hobo to his feet and says, "Home, Hobo." The dog licks her face, then slowly heads off. With every step to the left or right, he looks like he's going to lose his balance. Finally, he stumbles into a right turn and disappears from sight, and that's when Claudine leaves, ignoring us, like we never existed.

"You're welcome, Claudine," I say behind her back.

"Thanking you probably isn't on her mind, Benny,"

Jocko says. "If I were her, I'd be worried every day that Hobo might not show up at dismissal, which would mean he died."

"How does she know he'll make it home?" Beanie asks.

"She only lives a few houses down the street," I say.

Jocko smiles. "How do you know that?"

"I must've driven by with my dad one day and saw her out front. What does it matter?"

"I guess it doesn't," Jocko says, grinning stupidly at me.

NIGHT CRAWLER

In class, things aren't going too well with Sara, and right now I'd rather be in my after-school drawing class sketching cartoons.

Ms. D tries to help, telling everyone to let our minds "roam" on whatever images come to mind. "Free-associate," she says.

When we talk individually, Sara asks me to describe how a night crawler is different from a regular worm, so I repeat how in late spring my grandfather and I patrol his backyard with flashlights, trying to catch worms peeking out from their holes before they see the light and recoil.

"What do you do with them?"

"We use them for bait."

"You mean you stick a hook into them?"

I wonder how someone so smart can ask such a dumb question, but I say, "Yeah, they're usually very juicy."

She cringes, and I'm guessing that's what Caulfield means by an image being powerful. So I decide to tone things down or we'll end up writing about ballet shoes instead of night crawlers.

"Did you write a draft of the poem last night?" I ask.

"I focused more on jotting down nighttime images."

"Really?" I say, thinking this won't be too helpful. "Like what?"

"Like the sound of a railroad car, wet grass, a street-light, a baby crying." And she rattles off about five more. "What about you?" she asks.

"I actually wrote the whole poem last night."

She seems surprised and asks me to read it.

"'My grandpa and me go fishing, but first we get night crawlers, creepy little creatures with big noses. They look like fingers someone cut off as they crawl around. But we grab them and I don't mind getting all wet and dirty.'"

She's looking at my sheet of paper, pursing her lips like she just sucked on a lemon. "It kind of reads like sentences," she says, way too loudly, and I can feel Claudine eavesdropping. "Also," she adds, "we can't have the name

of the object in the poem. People are supposed to guess it."
She's right about that.

"But it's got poetry," I say, "the way I talk about them
having noses and compare them to fingers."

Maybe I'm crazy, but I'm sure she glances at Claudine
before saying, "That's good, but we're going to have line
breaks, right, and maybe rhyme?"

In fact, I had no intention of having line breaks. "Yeah,
sure," I say.

"I mean," she adds, "I thought we could make the
poem sound like the slurping noise night crawlers make
when they go in and out of their holes."

Slurping noise?

"We'll get it right," I say, "but maybe we should write
something we can take home and fiddle with."

So we write separately for a while, and I give her this:

My grandpa and me
go fishing but first
we capture them,
creepy little creatures with big noses.
They look like fingers someone cut off
as they crawl around. But we grab them
and I don't mind getting all wet and dirty.

Why mess with perfection? So all I do is get rid of the "night crawlers" and change "get" to "capture." Who cares where I break the lines?

Right before class ends, she slides a sheet over to me:

The last automobile of the night passes,
And I fall on a blanket of grass.
My left hand catches them coupling.
Rooted to the ground yet aspiring upward.
Anonymous.

I'm not too sure what I think of this, but at least it doesn't rhyme. "Really terrific, Sara," I say.

"You think so?"

"Yeah, it almost reads like a finished poem," and I'm not lying about that, though I can't make sense of that "Anonymous."

Ms. D interrupts us by saying, "Time's up. Why don't you work on each other's drafts tonight? Then on Friday, you can meet in pairs again, and on Monday we'll read them."

In the hall, I ask Beanie how he made out. He was paired with Bethany Briggs. "Okay, I guess."

"Just okay?"

"I don't think either one of us cares much."

"What are you writing on?"

Suddenly, Claudine's busybody voice invades my space. "You can't ask him that."

Beanie doesn't want to agree but knows she's right. "It *is* a kind of a contest, dude."

Claudine smiles, and before walking away, shakes her finger at me. "And don't think you're going to bully Sara into writing a prose poem."

Ah, so maybe Sara isn't a neutral. Maybe she's been turned to the Dark Side.

SAMUEL MORSE

It's hard to say when Claudine and I became enemies, but obviously our fates are linked, because she's been in my classes since first grade. She's taller than everyone, and unlike the rest of us, who are always slouching, thinking someone's making fun of us, she has the posture of a figure skater or gymnast. Also, she has so much confidence when she talks that she's very intimidating. You would think most kids would hate her, but girls buzz around her like she's the queen bee, and she usually ends up president of the class. She never gets the boy vote, but there are enough guys who are either scared of her or so used to her winning, they just don't care.

Why don't the boys like her? Probably because she's

always waiting for us to say something dumb, so she can pounce on us, proving her point at our expense. I imagine her staying up all night, eyes as big as Ping-Pong balls, anticipating some bonehead guy's response to the day's lesson, so she can get in his face. I should admire what Ms. D calls Claudine's "determination," but the Book has taught me there are other words for "determination," like "pushy, obnoxious, egotistical, bullheaded, intolerant, tyrannical"—well, you get the picture.

Claudine and I wouldn't battle so much if I zoned her out the way most guys do, but one of my traits is that I don't like being bullied or seeing others bullied. Another one of my traits is that I can argue you to death. You want to argue that the cafeteria pizza is great, I can counter with a hundred reasons why it isn't, even if it's my favorite meal. This so-called negative characteristic drives my mother nuts, but it's like I can't stop myself. I always see the other side of an argument. My mother thinks I'm going to be a lawyer. My father says I'm going to be a huge pain in the neck, though that's not the word he uses, and you don't need a thesaurus to guess it.

So, in a way, Claudine and I had no choice but to be enemies from day one, and school was our battlefield. I had my breakthrough in fifth grade. The teacher, Ms. Bright, assigned us a two-paragraph report on Samuel Morse. I already knew he had invented the telegraph, but I discovered he'd been a pretty good painter, too, so I wrote about that, thinking it would be more interesting. When my time came, I proudly recited my report, and right as I finished, Claudine's hand shot up. She's a sly one. Teachers would hate her if she said, "Benny's report is dumb because he missed Samuel Morse's most important contribution," or if she was smirking and sighing and shaking her head disgustedly as I spoke. But not Claudine. Even then, she had perfected this fake look of interest, a whole routine where she compliments you first before lowering the boom.

That day she said, "Benny makes many good points, but a man's real accomplishment is judged by how many lives he has changed, and *certainly* the telegraph and Morse code are more important than *mediocre* paintings." It was the way she emphasized "certainly" and "mediocre" that sent me over the edge.

"Why wouldn't painting be important?" I asked, surprising myself.

Fake concern again. "It's not unimportant. It's just not *as* important as the telegraph."

"So you're saying if I give a hand to some old guy who's fallen down and no one sees me, that's not as important as helping a hundred people on national TV?"

She was a bit baffled by that, and I was waiting for the

teacher to interrupt, but Ms. Bright seemed to be enjoying the conflict. After a long pause, Claudine said, "I would be glad you helped someone, but helping a hundred people is better."

"What if I was helping all those people so I'd be famous? What if I hated them all? Isn't the feeling behind something important? Maybe Morse hated creating the telegraph. Maybe he invented it to make money. Maybe he was laughing his head off as he watched people tapping away like a bunch of idiots."

Silence again. Then Claudine said, "Well, if Samuel Morse was such a great painter, why didn't anyone else mention it in their reports?"

I wanted to say, "Because everyone got their two paragraphs done, then didn't read the rest of the entry in the encyclopedia," but it was clear the class was liking this confrontation, so I didn't want to push them toward Claudine's side.

Rather than play her game, I pulled out a sheet of other facts on Morse's painting that I didn't have space to include. "Did you know," I said, "that the famous painter Washington Allston liked Morse's paintings so much, he took him to England, where Morse studied and was so good he was admitted to the Royal Academy?" And then I read from my notes. "'And there Morse studied the paintings of Michelangelo and created his masterpiece *Dying Hercules*.'" To be honest, I had never seen the painting and didn't really know how significant it was to be admitted to the Royal Academy, but all those facts seemed to stun Claudine, as if she had lunged forward with her sword and I had disarmed her. But she recovered enough to save face, saying, "Honestly, Benny, you didn't give those facts in your report. Now I may have to reconsider. The telegraph was Morse's most important contribution, but maybe his paintings were *equally* as important."

Too late, Claudine, I thought, and I was about to go for the jugular when Ms. Bright came to her rescue, saying, "It's clear we've learned two things today: First, great people are often multitalented; second, two different views on those people can be *equally* correct." Had she gone over to the Dark Side too?

What's important is that after that day, I became a legend with the boys. I had stood up for every guy who had been turned into a donkey by Claudine. But I had also alienated her until death do us part. The difference was that now *she* had to be on top of her game, because instead of feeling sick to my stomach every time I spoke in class, I thought, *Bring it on, girl.*

Now all I have to do is stop blushing when she talks to me.

OSTRICHES AND PIGEONS

Thursday afternoons I go to my grandfather's house and we work on language. It's something he looks forward to. That and watching sports on TV. Crash used to come, until he freaked out and I found him in the kitchen crying. I was doing opposites with my grandfather, where I say a word, show him its picture, then ask him to say the opposite. It's something any first grader can do, but after the stroke it would've been easier for my grandfather to slip on a pair of ballet shoes and walk on a tightrope across the gorge at Niagara Falls with a four-hundred-pound gorilla on his back.

That day he was doing okay, but after about the tenth opposite, I saw him struggling. When this happens, as tough as he is, he looks like he's about five years old. He becomes very frustrated and sad, and I wish I could open his skull and repair the connections that got messed up.

Because he was struggling, I shifted to another word exercise, but he was spent by then, and he got emotional, holding Crash's hand and slowly rubbing it, saying what a good boy he was. His PT Boat hat was turned a bit sideways, so Crash straightened it, and when he did, my grandfather's eyes welled up. Crash kind of lost it and ran into the kitchen. My grandfather looked a little perplexed, but I distracted him by talking about the Patriots, which always works.

Today, though, is going well. We start naming things around the house: a sugar bowl, a Patriots calendar, a clock on the wall. Then I grab a box containing pictures of ten kinds of birds, and they aren't the easiest ones to recognize. My father told me researchers discovered that sometimes stroke patients recover faster by challenging their brains, moving from harder pictures and words to easier ones instead of vice versa. Grandpa does great today on the birds, though ostriches and pigeons always throw him. I tell him that whenever he sees a pigeon, he should think of crap, because that's all they do. He laughs loudly and says, "How's Crap doing, anyway?"

"It's Crash, Grandpa."

"That's what I said."

"The hawk hasn't come back, so he's just being his usual nasty self."

"Yeah, he's a piece of work, but I guess all Alvarez boys are."

"What do you mean?"

"We're all pains in the butt." Then he lowers his voice and looks around. "I don't want her"—meaning Gloria— "to hear that. I want her to think she married a Greek god."

Not much chance of that happening, I think. "You know, my mom says I'm negative."

"A wonderful woman, your mom. Two chances, and I couldn't get one like her." Gloria's sitting in the other room, watching some religious TV show, so I ask Grandpa to lower his voice. That's another Alvarez trait. You always know when we're around.

"She's great, Grandpa, but all that 'don't sweat the small stuff' garbage and those lists she posts all over the house wear me down."

"What lists?" And then I remember Grandpa hasn't been able to read the newest ones.

"Mostly quotes from famous people saying life's wonderful. I don't need a dumb movie star to tell me that."

"Real nonsense, huh?"

"Yeah."

"You think the world's a lousy place, Benny?"

"Don't you ever watch TV, Grandpa, or pay attention to how people treat one another?"

"Hmmmm," he says.

"The way I see it, it's best to think of the worst that can happen. Then you're never disappointed. Whatever goes down is better than what you expected."

He squints at me. "Never get hurt that way, do you?"

"You bet," I say, proud that Grandpa sees the genius of my approach.

"Don't really live, though, either."

Because he can be as contrary as the rest of us, I wonder if he's teasing me with that comment, so I don't answer. Instead, we move to another word game, then go to the living room, where we putt balls into a Dixie cup for about a half hour, every once in a while moving the cup farther away. Gloria has fallen asleep on the couch, so we turn off the TV right as some guy with greasy black hair combed back like Dracula and wearing a shiny gray suit and red tie explains that the Devil is everywhere, even at your local bowling alley.

"A bunch of screwballs," Grandpa says. "Devils don't bowl. Like your dad says, they live in Washington and make laws."

That's the weird thing about Grandpa. One minute he can't tell you what an ostrich is, the next minute he makes complete sense.

"Don't talk so loud," I say, "or you'll wake up Gloria."

"You could shoot a gun next to that woman and she wouldn't wake up."

"Probably not a good idea, Grandpa."

"You're a real card, Benny. You're going to be famous someday."

Personally, I just want to make it through Becky Walters's party without getting insulted by Claudine or having to dance.

ZOMBIES

The next day I talk to Jocko and Beanie about my grandfather's stroke.

"I wouldn't want to deal with that," Beanie says. "My pops"—that's what he calls his grandfather—"has cancer, and he says if things get bad to buy him a good box of cigars, then strand him in the middle of the ocean on a little rowboat."

"That's pretty harsh," Jocko says.

"Not really," I say. "He's smoking his favorite cigar, watching a great sunset. It's better than rotting away in a hospital."

"Only you could see it that way," Jocko says.

"Well, how would *you* see it?" I ask, a bit annoyed.

"I'd want to be surrounded by my family. The other way seems kind of selfish."

"Selfish?" Beanie says, obviously mad that Jocko is calling his pops selfish. Then he tells Jocko he's been acting a little weird lately, kind of touchy-feely, butting in when it's none of his business.

"Weird? Touchy-feely?"

"Yeah, you're talking like an adult."

"That's a whack idea."

"He's kind of right," I say.

Jocko's shaking his head, and as I said, he's very big and very strong, so we don't want to get him mad.

"Maybe 'adult' wasn't the right word," I say, as if Beanie had called him a wood louse or a maggot.

"If Beanie says 'adult,' then it's 'adult.' Beanie *always* uses the right word."

"What I'm saying," Beanie adds, "is that lately, you've been overly kind to everyone."

"Overly kind?"

"Yeah, like understanding."

I guess it's a good thing to be called kind and understanding, but Jocko isn't very happy, so I come to Beanie's aid.

"He has a point, dude. Do you remember what you said when Big Joe tripped Joey Pappas at recess? You said, 'You have to wonder what's going on at Big Joe's house for him to do that.'"

"What's wrong with that?"

"The old Jocko would've said, 'That guy needs a good beat down.' The old Jocko wouldn't have been thinking about Big Joe's home life. Big Joe's an idiot. It's pretty simple."

"You guys are whacked," Jocko says.

I'm angry now, so I decide to give him both barrels. "If I ask you one more thing, you promise not to get mad?"

He's looking a little nervous.

"Are you going out with Becky?"

"Going out?"

"Twice last week you said you couldn't shoot hoops. One day you said you had too much homework. The second day you had extra soccer practice."

"I did."

Now I have him. "One of those days Beanie saw you at the toy store with Becky; the other, I saw you and Becky riding bikes."

"I didn't want to deal with your garbage. We're just friends, so what am I supposed to do, ask you two to come along?"

"I'm not criticizing," I say.

Jocko smirks. "Yeah, right. You know, Benny, I've been

waiting to use a word for a while, and now it fits. I really find you *beleaguering*, and I'm not even going to make you guys guess, because I checked its origins. It's worse than being annoyed or irritated. It has to do with being in an actual exhausting battle with someone, and after spending ten minutes with your negative attitude, I feel like someone kicked me in the privates. I almost sympathize with Claudine."

"Ouch!" Beanie says.

"It's true, man. You act like you don't know why that girl dislikes you."

"But I do," I say, and I go through the Samuel Morse story.

"Yeah, yeah, I've heard that one and normally let it slide, but it wasn't fifth grade, dude, it was last year. We were reading some novel about a girl in Tennessee whose father left her, so she ran away and lived in the woods with her dog. If you remember, Claudine stood up for her, and then you got diarrhea of the mouth and ripped into the girl in the book, saying she was a loser and that her father was something else I don't remember."

"A coward," Benny interjects.

"Yeah," Jocko continues, "and we were all hoping you'd just shut up, because most people knew Claudine's dad had split the week after her parents had that big fight outside school."

I do remember that.

"So she hates you, man. Think about it. You're depressed because your dad leaves. You're embarrassed because your parents are swearing at each other in front of your friends and teachers, and then some dude tells you your father's a loser."

"I didn't say that."

"He's right," Beanie says. "He said the character was a loser, not her father."

"Duh, you guys are dense."

"Why didn't you tell me this back then?"

"I don't know, maybe because she can get on my nerves too. I'm not saying I don't have your back. I'm just saying you can be a real jerk."

I don't know what to say, so I try making a joke. "My grandpa says I'm a card. Why don't we go with that?"

Jocko smiles. "Yeah, you're a card, all right. The Old Maid."

"No," Beanie says, "he's that card in Monopoly that says 'Go to jail. Do not pass Go or collect two hundred dollars.'" Then Beanie grabs the Book from his back pocket and looks up the word "card." "Here it is: a clown, an eccentric, a freak, a nut, an oddball, a weirdo, a zombie."

"I rest my case," Jocko says, then holds out his arms and stumbles toward me like a hungry zombie.

HECTOR THE MOUSE

I've never understood Jocko's obsession with vampire-zombie-werewolf books. They aren't even scary anymore, though I'm surprised schools let kids read them. When I was in fourth grade, I found this great book in the school library about three kids who live in the city, and in one scene the bully gets drunk. When a mom heard about that, she complained, and the school removed the book. I guess they were afraid we'd read it and start drinking, even though the drunk kid was a loser. Meanwhile, at the same school, there were at least fifty vampire books, a few where people get their heads cut off or even get eaten. So I guess they're saying it's better to be a cannibal than a drunk? I ranted on this in class one day when we were talking about censorship, and Ms. D said, "That's one way of looking at it, Benny." Whenever someone says that, what they're really saying is "That's really negative, Benny, and I'd rather not deal with your nonsense today."

Right now, my mother's saying the same thing about my take on Crash's response to a mouse that has suddenly appeared in the basement. My father's standing in the kitchen, wearing his winter boots, and two plastic mouse-traps are opened on the counter in front of him. He has a butter knife in one hand, dipping its tip into a jar of peanut butter, then spreading a little on the traps.

I guess when he was cleaning his workroom, he scared a mouse from its hiding place, so now it's wandering around the basement.

"Crazy little bugger," my father says. "I thought he'd see me, then hide, but I made about thirty trips, and every time, he's bouncing off the baseboards like a drunk."

My mother is trying not to laugh at my father's boots.

"It's not funny, Margaret. I didn't see you going down to help."

"I would've called a professional," my mother says.

"And spend a fortune?"

"What's a Dumpster doing outside the house?" I ask.

"What grade are you in, Benny? A Dumpster, thirty trips from the basement. Get it?"

"Your father finally decided to toss all the junk the previous owners left," my mother says. "I told him to wait until the mouse left."

"Or maybe I should've tried to reason with him, like Crash."

"Like Crash?"

"Yeah," my father says. "He saw me come in with the mousetraps, so he's downstairs and says he won't let anyone kill it."

"He's watching too much of that Animal Planet channel," I say.

"Bingo," my father says, spreading on more peanut butter.

"Why peanut butter?" I ask.

"The smart ones can steal cheese," my father says, "but they've got to stick their heads in the trap to get the peanut butter, and then," and he lets one of the traps snap shut.

"Isn't there another way?" my mother says.

"Why don't you ask the mouse whisperer?" my father says, meaning Crash.

"It's nature," I say. "Dad gave it enough chances."

"I certainly tried to warn it."

"Yes," my mother says. "He put on those heavy boots, and every time he went downstairs, he stomped hard and growled like a bear."

I wish I had been home to hear that.

"And the varmint still walked right past me like we were of the same species. And let me tell you about mice, Benny, they aren't cute."

"How do you plan to get Crash up here?" I ask.

"An idea that's still percolating," my father says, finishing his job.

My mother is shaking her head at the traps. "You're wasting your time with those. Crash won't allow it."

"Crash is nine years old," my father says.

"Then I won't allow it. He has a right to his beliefs. He's a sensitive soul."

"Your 'sensitive soul' is going to give his father a heart attack. I'm too old for this, Margaret."

"Not appropriate, Colin," she says. "His beliefs are important."

"What if he believes he should add rat poison to our scrambled eggs?" I offer.

"Apt comparison, Benny," my father says.

"Completely exaggerated," my mother says.

"Then what if he decides homework should no longer be part of school?"

"Don't start, Benny."

"I'm just saying, Mom, that he's a kid and has to learn he's not the boss."

"That's one way of looking at it, but it's not the choice we're making."

At this point, it's clear that the garbage will be the next location of the mousetraps. Here's the thing I've never understood about the Alvarez boys. We'll battle to the death if we believe in something, yet we always end up doing what my mother or Irene wants. It's like some Alvarez wimp five centuries ago passed on a defective gene.

"So what do we do?" my father asks. "I'm not putting on these boots every time I go downstairs." I guess he's afraid the mouse is going to bite his big toe.

"Let me talk to Crash," I say, and head toward the basement. When I open the door, I see him sitting on the bottom step.

"Don't you think you should move up a few?" I say.

"He won't hurt me."

"How do you know it's a he?"

"Don't start, Benny Alvarez."

"Okay, Mom."

"You know what I mean," he says.

I take a few steps at a time, and when I reach the bottom, I sit behind him, peering around the corner. Finally, I locate the mouse, sniffing around the leg of our large pool table. I thought mice ran fast, but this little hairy thing kind of waddles toward the wall. Then he creeps alongside it, turns, and retraces his steps.

"Does he have a name?"

"Hector."

Might as well destroy those traps, Dad. The mouse has now become a human being.

"You want to talk?"

"No, I've been listening to you all babble upstairs. Call Aldo."

"What?"

"Call Aldo."

When I return to the kitchen, my mother's holding the phone. "We heard him."

I call my sister, who's at a girl friend's house. She says Aldo is out of town with his father, looking at colleges, but she'll try to locate him. About ten minutes later Aldo is on the phone with Crash. Fifteen minutes later, Crash comes upstairs. "Aldo will take care of it tomorrow."

"What's the plan?" my father asks.

"I'm sleeping on the pool table tonight," Crash says, "and you have to promise you won't kill him when I'm at school."

My father's fingering the mousetraps.

"He promises," my mother says. "I'll get your sleeping bag."

Crash seems pacified. "His name's Hector," he tells my father.

"Like the Greek hero?"

"No, like Hector the Mouse."

Things calm down a bit after that. We all have dinner; then Crash breaks off some chunks of cheese for Hector.

"Why don't we invite him to dinner?" I say. "A little turkey and gravy would be tasty. Maybe he can bring his family."

"Benny," my mother says.

"He's probably too full from all that cheese Crash fed him," my father adds. "But there's always dessert. What's for dessert today, Margaret? Cheesecake?"

Irene is helping my mother clean up. "Don't listen to them, Crash. Aldo will be here tomorrow."

"Yeah," I say, "Aldo will probably leash it, then tie it to his drum set. Hector could be the Cro-Magnons' mascot."

"Enough," my mother says. "You guys have had your fun."

And we have, though I pay for it much, much later. At about two a.m., I wake up, thinking about Crash in the basement all by himself, too on guard to sleep. "Darn it, Crash," I say. I fall out of bed and search the closet for my sleeping bag. The next thing I know, I'm lying next to Crash on the pool table.

"You think it will collapse?" he asks.

"Not this monstrosity, but I'll sleep on the floor if you want."

"You'd do that for me?"

"What could happen?"

"No, just stay here, but turn off the lights, okay?"

I slide off the pool table, flip the light switch by the stairs, then feel my way back, hoping not to step on anything squishy.

After we get settled, Crash says, "Good night, Benny," and I say, "Good night, Crash," and then he says, "Good night, Hector."

I'm relieved when there's no reply.

A. J. LOGOS

Jocko, Beanie, and I are outside school again, hanging around the bike rack. It's a beautiful day, but the sun is stinging my eyes, and the whole right side of my body hurts from sleeping on the pool table. Added to that, Crash tossed and turned all night, farting.

"Dude, what happened to you?" Beanie asks.

"Yeah," Jocko says. "You look like someone beat you with a baseball bat."

"Crash happened to me," I say, and I relate the mouse story.

"He's a strange little dude," Beanie says.

"I think he's cool," Jocko says.

"'Scary' is a better word," I say.

"No, your dad's the scary one."

"Scary" isn't a word I'd associate with my father.

"You never know what he's going to say," Jocko adds.

"What do you mean?" I ask, hoping my father doesn't blurt out embarrassing things around them.

"Not bad things," Jocko says, "just unexpected things, like you might ask him what kind of day he's having, and he'll say, 'Better than the starving peasants in Afghanistan,' or I'll ask to borrow a pen, and he'll say, 'Fine, but I know where you live.'"

I'm relieved to hear it was just his usual teasing.

"I'm not criticizing," Jocko says. "At least it's not boring at your house."

"No," I say, "there's always some kind of hullaballoo."

"You're kidding, right?" Beanie asks.

"What?"

"That's sooooo easy, dude."

"Au contraire."

"Only one a day," Jocko says.

"Well, I'll expect you to guess where the word comes from. That's part of it."

"Ah, the bar is being raised higher," Jocko says.

"You guys are giving me a headache," Beanie says, "but speaking about the Book, I found out yesterday that A. J. Logos is a woman, and that A. J. Logos isn't even her name."

"Where did you see that?" I ask.

"My dad told me *logos* is the Greek word for 'word,' and the book is all about words, so I checked out A. J. Logos on Google."

"And . . ."

"She's an eighty-year-old librarian from Enid, Oklahoma."

"You're kidding, right?" Jocko says, and I can relate to his shock. I guess it's not that important that A. J. Logos isn't a guy, but an eighty-year-old woman librarian? It's a kind of betrayal.

"Is it just me," I say, "or is it creepy we're obsessed with a book written by an old lady?"

"I don't think 'creepy's' the word," Jocko says, and before he can finish his thought, Beanie's opening the Book.

"'Creepy: awful, disgusting, disturbing, ghoulish . . .'"

"Okay, okay, I get it," I say.

"There *is* something I didn't mention," Beanie says. "When she wrote the book, she was in her twenties."

Jocko whacks Beanie alongside the head.

"Hey, man, that hurts."

"He oughta smack you again," I say. "Why didn't you mention that before? For all we know, A. J. Logos could've looked like Ms. D when she was in her twenties."

"Maybe I can find her picture," Beanie says.

"Not necessary," I say. "We'll take for granted she was hot."

"Agreed," Jocko says.

"Yeah, but this proves again you can't trust anyone or anything anymore. People are always running scams."

"How does what Beanie said prove that?" Jocko says, rolling his eyes.

I'm about to explain my logic when one of the teachers' aides yells for us to come in.

NIGHT CRAWLER REVISITED

I'm dreading the last twenty minutes of Ms. D's class, because Sara's been eyeballing me strangely since I sat down. She has a look falling somewhere between fear and disgust. One thing that's obvious is that she is no longer a neutral but now is under the spell of Wicked Witch Claudine. Fortunately, between dinner and bedtime I had a chance to rewrite my poem, forcing in a few of her images:

Night Crawler

My grandpa and me
go fishing, but first
we wait until the last

car goes home, then
we capture them,
creepy little creatures with big noses,
half out of holes.
They look like fingers someone cut off
but we grab them, and I don't mind
getting wet and dirty.

Of course my real version is in sentences, but I don't want to end up with Sara's pen stuck in my forehead.

"You like it?" I ask.

She waits a long while, then says, "Very much, Benny, but why did you leave out the 'anonymous'?"

"Because I don't know what it means."

"Worms are anonymous because they all look alike," she says.

"But they don't. Some are short, some long, some redder than others."

She's not going to let this go. "But they all squirm and have a similar shape. It's not like some have eyes and some don't, or that some look like grasshoppers."

"True," I say, though I'm still a bit lost. "Can I see your version?" And she passes over a sheet of paper with pink borders.

Night Crawler

The last automobile of night passes.
I drop to my knees on a blanket of wet grass.
Silence,
except for the opening and closing
of tiny dark doors.
Flashlight in my right hand,
creatures scatter under its enormous eye,
or I catch them, half out of holes,
damp noses breaking the surface.
Anonymous creatures, soft-bellied fragments,
I gladly crawl on grass
for a handful of them.

I can't say I know everything that's going on in this poem, but it's clear I'm out of my league. This is either a great poem or unintelligible, but one thing I've learned from six years of school is that people like poems they can't understand.

"What happened to my grandfather?" I ask.

She looks a bit hurt. "That's all you can say?"

"No, it certainly sounds a lot better than mine, but I thought the poem was about my grandfather and me."

"It's supposed to focus on an object. Remember?"

We must be raising our voices, because kids are looking at us, one being Claudine.

"Mind your own business, Claudine," I want to yell.

"I thought you'd put your grandfather back in later," Sara says. "I mean, I don't even know him."

"Can I ask you why you broke the lines where you did?" I ask.

"I read and reread the poem about a hundred times, trying different line breaks, until the poem sounded right. You know what I mean?"

Actually, I wrote my version over a half-hour span while I was eating popcorn and watching reruns of *Looney Tunes*. "Yeah, it takes a while to get the sound right," I say.

"I didn't expect you to use my version, Benny. I figured you'd tinker with it over the weekend."

"So you don't mind me rewriting it?"

"As long as I can see it before you read it."

"*Me* read it?"

"I can't do it, Benny. I get too nervous."

"And I don't?"

"Well, you never *look* nervous. You're always talking and arguing in class."

I'm trying to decide whether this is a compliment. "Okay," I say. "I'll read it and I'll email you my revision on Sunday."

As we begin to exchange email addresses, Ms. D says, "Time to finish. On Monday we'll try to stump Mr. Jones and the whole class. Remember, I expect your poems to be neatly typed, and they must be a group effort." She looks at Paige when she says this.

Suddenly, Claudine speaks up. Her hair's hanging loose, and it seems to change to various hues of red when the sun, which is streaming through our windows, strikes it. "These poems have to be verse poems, right?"

Knowing she'd try this, I actually wrote down Caulfield's exact instructions. But before I can speak, Ms. D says, "Mr. Jones said poems in verse *or* sentences, Claudine. We must respect that."

Boy, is Claudine mad. "Well, that's stupid."

Ms. D seems a bit surprised, and the whole class momentarily freezes.

"Nevertheless, Claudine," Ms. D says, "those are the rules we agreed upon." Then she shoos us out of the room.

At recess Big Joe approaches me, and I'm thinking he's going to sit on me for ten minutes for "bugging" Claudine.

"I think you're a jerk, Benny," he says, "but it's hard enough to write a stupid poem without thinking about the junk Claudine's freaking over."

I'm wondering whether I should call him a jerk too before speaking. Maybe this is Big-Joe-speak.

"Thanks, Joe," I say.

"Don't thank me. You're still a jerk. All the guys feel the same way."

"That I'm a jerk?"

"No, about the poetry stuff."

"Well, Joe," I say, like I'm accepting the nomination for class president, "tell them I'll do my best on Monday to represent them."

"Huh?"

"Just tell them thanks."

BALD AS THE BEHIND OF A CHIMPANZEE

I go right to soccer practice after school, then toss the football with Jocko for a while, so I'm not home until five thirty. Aldo's Cro-Magnon car is in the driveway. I enter the house to the smell of chicken soup and see Irene toiling in the kitchen. She makes incredible chicken soup, and she always bakes her own bread, continually brushing butter on its crust until it glows in the oven. My father and grandfather are sitting at the granite table by the window, and my mother has the recliner kicked back, reading a novel and enjoying her night off. My father has offered to cook dinner every night, but fortunately, she declines. "Fortunately," because the only meals he can't ruin are grilled cheese and tuna fish sandwiches. Sometime he gets adventurous and combines the two, making a grilled-cheese-tuna-fish sandwich with rye bread. Whoop-de-do!

"Hi, sweetie," my mother says.

"Hi, Mom," I reply, then greet my father and grandfather. "I'm afraid to ask, but where are Crash and Aldo?"

"You won't recognize Aldo, anyway," my father says.

Irene sighs.

"Why's that?"

"He shaved his head."

I can't decide whether my father's happy or angry about this.

"You mean he's bald?"

"As bald as the behind of a chimpanzee," my grandfather says.

"Why did he do that?"

"First," Irene says, "he's not as bald as what Grandpa says. He got a buzz cut."

"There goes the caveman look," I say, pretending to be serious.

"I don't think Aldo cares what anyone thinks, Benny," Irene says, and I suddenly realize that's why she's fallen for him. The only other guys I know who don't care what people think are my father, my grandfather, Crash, and me. It won't be a big leap for her to move right in with him.

Irene is seldom mad, but she's close to it now. "You guys don't like it when he has long hair, and you don't like it when he has short hair."

Suddenly, a voice penetrates the kitchen floor. "We can hear you," Aldo yells.

An embarrassing silence follows, until my father responds with "We love you, Aldo."

"Ditto, Mr. Alvarez" comes back through the floor.

"You gotta like that kid," my grandfather says, "even if he doesn't have a behind."

Even my mother laughs at that.

"He's just skinny, Grandpa," Irene says.

"Come here, kiddo," he says, and when Irene joins him, he hugs her. "You and your mom are diamonds in the r-r-r . . . ," and he's having trouble finishing the sentence until my father says, "Rough." "Yeah," Grandfather says, "Bilbo's lucky to have you."

"It's Aldo, Grandpa."

"What kind of name is that?" he asks for about the hundredth time.

"It's Old German," Irene says.

"Really," my father says, intrigued by this discovery. "I thought he was Italian."

"Better German than Italian," Grandfather says, pronouncing the *I* in "Italian" like "eye."

"Inappropriate, Kieran," my mother says, never looking up from her book.

A few minutes later Aldo and Crash appear in the
kitchen, holding an empty plastic half-gallon milk bottle
with a yellow contraption screwed to its mouth. Inside the
container, Hector lies. You'd think he'd be going ballistic,
but he seems relaxed, almost half asleep.

"Oooooh," Irene says.

"He's a little thing," my mother adds, lifting herself off
the recliner. "He can't escape, can he?"

My father reaches for a poker next to the woodstove
and brandishes it like a sword. "I will defend you to the
death, Margaret."

Aldo, contrary to what certain Alvarez boys say, is
not really bald. He seems unfazed by all this nuttiness,
explaining how the trap works. "You place some goodies
in the bottle"—I can see pieces of cheese and ground-
up peanuts—"then screw this gadget on. Eventually the
mouse crawls in and you close off part of the opening,
so he can't squeeze through. You can release him then,
but that's inhumane. It's better to let him eat for a while,
so he gets tired and lazy instead of flipping out in the
bottle."

"We wouldn't want to upset him," my father says. "So
what's the plan now?"

"Crash and I are going to free him at the lake by the Little League field."

My father surprises me by saying, "Mind if I come?"

Aldo looks to Crash for an answer.

"You promise not to make jokes?"

"Promise," my father says.

"You want to come, Benny?"

"No thanks, Crash. I'm going to help Irene make dinner."

"How about you, Grandpa?"

"It'll take me a half hour to get to the front door," he says, not bothered in the least by this admission.

"That's okay, Grandpa; we're in no hurry."

"Just don't take too long," Irene says. "The bread tastes best right out of the oven."

They're about to leave when Aldo turns to my grandfather. "Mr. Alvarez?"

"Call me Grandpa, Bilbo."

"Really?"

"Sure—you'll be part of the family before you know it."

"Inappropriate, Grandpa," Irene says, blushing.

"It's true, kiddo, you learn something after eighty-five years." Then he looks at Aldo, waiting for his question.

"What's this stuff about my behind?" Aldo seems genuinely concerned about this physical deformity.

115

"That's a discussion for you and Irene," my mother interrupts, trying her best to get everyone out the door. My father's the last one to leave, but before he does, my mother pulls him aside and kisses him on the cheek. "I love you," she whispers, thinking no one can hear her. My father smiles and says, "Up, up, and away."

After the door closes, my mother says she needs to discuss something with me. I'd like to think she wants to compliment me on being an attractive, intelligent, and generally speaking superior individual, but that's probably wishful thinking.

"I have to talk to you about Becky Walters's party."

"Sure," I say.

"Becky's mother asked if I'd help chaperone it. She wants one of the boys' mothers to be there."

"Aren't you busy enough with work?"

"You don't want me to go?"

"It's my first real party."

"Should I tell her no, then?"

"What do you plan to do there?"

"Help out."

"You promise not to dance or give any of the guys a tough time?"

"You think I'm an idiot, Benny?"

"No, but I don't want everyone, especially Claudine,

116

wondering how such a nice woman like you ended up with me."

"That's a little dramatic."

Irene's been listening but doesn't say anything until now. "What're you worried about, Benny? These parties aren't a big deal." She goes over to the soup and starts stirring it. "Is it the dancing?"

"No, because I'm not going to dance."

"Trust me, no seventh-grade girl will ask you, anyway," Irene says.

"Especially the ones in my class. They hate me."

"I doubt that, Benny," my mother says.

"You haven't met Paige or Claudine."

"I've certainly heard enough about the latter."

"Well, it's kind of gotten worse with this poetry thing we're doing," I say. Then I explain the whole prose poem/verse poem battle.

"A conflict like that isn't going to make someone hate you," my mother says.

Irene laughs. "You haven't been in middle school for a while, Mom."

Irene's right, and I wonder if Claudine even cares about poetry, or if it's just another chance to stick it to Benny.

"You sure you're not describing your own motives? You can be very argumentative."

At least she didn't say negative.

"See, that's what I'm worried about. You'll side with the girls, and the next thing I know you'll be sipping punch and feasting on cheese and crackers with Claudine."

"Actually, Becky's mom is having it catered, and you can't expect me to ignore a certain group of guests. Claudine is a beautiful girl. Have you ever seen her?" my mother asks Irene.

"Yes, she's very cute."

"What does that have to do with anything?"

They both kind of smile, and I know it's time to end this conversation.

"Just go, Mom, but don't ask me to dance and don't mention my 'negativity.'"

"I'd never do that, though I'd love to dance with you," she says. And she places my arms in the proper position, leading me around the kitchen, humming some tune she has stuck in her head from a hundred years ago. I'm stumbling and dizzy and don't understand why anyone would want to dance like this. Whenever I've seen people slow dancing on TV, they stay in one place, swaying. Then she passes me on to Irene, and they're having a grand old time until I say, "I think the bread's burning," which ends this fiasco.

OUR "FRIENDLY" POETRY EXERCISE

Monday comes way too slowly, because I work all weekend to finish the night crawler poem. I'm excited about stumping everyone while showing Claudine you can write a good poem without rhymes or line breaks. I'm up so late Sunday that I'm half asleep when Jocko and Beanie ring the doorbell.

"My dad's taking me today," I say.

Beanie's sitting on his BMX, wearing what looks like a leather beret.

"What's that?" I say. "Halloween's two weeks away."

"It's poetry day. I'm looking poetic."

"No, you're looking stupid," Jocko says.

119

I agree with Jocko and watch as they turn their bikes around and speed off.

Halfway to school, my father gets cut off by a woman in a Volvo.

"Late for Pilates?" he says, then suggests that the roads are crawling with "ignoramuses," and this gets him going. "You ever wonder, Benny, why the plural of 'ignoramus' isn't 'ignorami'? I mean, the plural of 'octopus' is 'octopi.'"

"Not something I've thought about lately," I say.

"I'm serious. You're the one who's supposed to dig words."

"Dig" is not a word I've heard him use before. "Appreciate" fits that bald head and those wire-rimmed glasses better.

"The plural of 'octopus' comes from Latin, right?"

"Yeah, the deadest of dead languages."

"Don't tell Claudine that."

"The girl you think is tormenting you?"

"No, the girl I'm sure is tormenting me."

"Is she pretty?"

"Why does everyone harp on that?"

"Just asking. Well, you'll get your way today. You happy with your poem?"

"Yeah, it's about Grandpa and me getting night crawlers."

"You want to read it to me now?"

"Maybe tonight."

"Darn," he says as we pass the elementary school where Crash goes. "Here's another mindless citizen, the woman who double-parks to drop off her kids."

"Especially when the kids take five minutes to find their backpacks in the backseat."

"Well said, Benny, but you know what your mom would say," and we sing in one voice, "'There're two ways to look at this situation.'" Then he adds, "She actually believes people have reasons for doing inane things."

"What blows me away," I say, "is that she's never disappointed by anything, even if it's completely unexpected."

"Yeah, at least the Alvarez boys are always prepared for a horror show, almost disappointed when it doesn't happen." He's smiling again, and I can't decide how serious he is.

Finally the woman who's double-parked moves on, and we pass the elementary school. "Just think," I say, "right now Crash is probably ruining some poor teacher's day."

"But they love him. He's like the neighborhood dog that barks all day, but you know he just needs to be petted. Last year, his teacher called him 'adorable.'"

"Crash?"

"That's what she said."

"Did they ever say that about me?"

"Sad to say, no, Benny. The word they used most often was 'confrontational.' But this new teacher likes you, and you know that being 'confrontational' is fine with me, as long as you aren't disrespectful."

We pull up to my school's entrance right before classes start. I get through homeroom, but later, it's hard to concentrate in Mr. Congo's class, even though he has his pep back and is teaching a new concept. I keep opening my folder and rereading the night crawler poem. Claudine's doing the same with her poem, and when she looks up, I want to challenge her to an arm wrestle, ending our conflict once and for all.

When Mr. Congo's class is over, I hang around so I won't bump into Claudine in the hall. Everything's going fine until I notice Sara hovering outside Ms. D's classroom. There's something different about her. She's all dressed up, wearing a short blue skirt and powder-blue sweater. Snug around her neck is a necklace made from small, blue, shiny stones. She looks worried.

"You were supposed to email me," she says.

I completely forgot. I didn't even check my account over the weekend.

"Oh, man, I'm really sorry." So I hand her a copy of the poem before we take our normal seats, with her sitting in a group behind me.

Caulfield's in his lifeguard position, looking spiffy in jeans, a white dress shirt, a tweed sports coat, and black penny loafers with copper pennies staring out from the slits. He looks more like a lawyer than a poet.

But here's the odd part. Ms. D is also sitting on the desk with her feet up on a chair, so their thighs are almost touching, and I'm wondering how much weight this desk can hold. She's dressed in light-green slacks and a white short-sleeve blouse, and I can smell her perfume from a mile away. I look around the room and notice almost every girl has dressed up for this event. Before I refocus on Caulfield and Ms. D, I turn to see Sara gaping at me. I give her a "Wassup?" motion with my hands, and when she points to our poem, I realize I forgot to rewrite her copy in line breaks. That was my plan: to write mine in prose, and hers in verse. Who would know the difference when I read it?

Caulfield stands, spreading his hands like a preacher. He solemnly says, "I have gathered you today to celebrate the Word." Then he and Ms. D break out laughing.

"Seriously, though," he says. "I'm looking forward to us guessing the titles of your poems, and I've brought some prizes." Then he holds up a few books, all of which are written by him.

Next it's Ms. D's turn, and she explains her complicated

way of choosing the order of readers.

Paige goes first, with Big Joe shuffling behind her toward the front of the classroom. When they get settled, he jams his hands in his front pockets and stares at the ceiling, while Paige glares at everyone, as if to say, "I'm going to read my poem, and if you don't like it, I'm going to smack you."

"Should I explain the poem," she asks Caulfield, "or just read it?"

"No, no explanations. The poem should speak for itself."

Paige takes a deep breath, followed by:

"The king of every party,
I'm dragged by a white worm
and loved by everyone.
I'm a punching bag,
an enemy of tiny birds.
Grab me tightly, and
don't let go."

"Ah," Caulfield says, "read it once more."

"You want to read it, Joe?" she asks, trying to be polite.

"Read what?" he says, and the class laughs. Then Paige recites the poem again.

Meanwhile, I look at Beanie and mouth the word "balloon." Forgetting to wait for us, Caulfield says the same thing, then gives a short lecture on a few of the images. Most kids couldn't care less about his analysis, though I agree that comparing a string to a white worm is very cool.

A few groups follow Paige and Big Joe, and we all have a pretty easy time guessing the titles. My favorite is Beanie and Bethany's poem:

"I take the sun and
turn it into shade.
Winter stinks! Summer rocks!
And I'm here to prove it.
Unlike sunscreen, everyone loves me,
though there are more kinds of me's
than bathing suits.
I'm a cheap mirror,
I'm mainly worn by teens and rock stars."

Before anyone can guess the title, Beanie says, "It's sunglasses. Get it?"

We all laugh, and Caulfield almost faints with excitement at "Summer rocks!" but I like the idea of a thousand little mirrors staring up at me as I walk down the beach. I wouldn't have thought of that.

Now there're only two groups left, Claudine and Bob Langley and Sara and me. Claudine and Bob are up first. Claudine is looking a bit wild, her curly red hair puffed out at the sides, like she just stuck her finger in a light socket. She's wearing a red top and tight black jeans. But it's her shoes that get your attention, bright red and pointy, like she's auditioning for *The Wizard of Oz*. She's staring at everyone very seriously while Bob, in baggy jeans and a Red Sox T-shirt, looks like he'd rather be shooting hoops. I'm waiting for Claudine to begin reading, but she throws me a curve by reciting from memory:

> *"Boundaries of water,*
> *enclosing miniatures of the world—*
> *houses, lawns, and tiny trees.*
> *And then the house trembles—*
> *currents of snow made*
> *by your shaking hand."*

Caulfield is clearly puzzled by the poem, so he asks us for help, but we don't have a clue. He has to respond in some way, so he says, "Very intense, Claudine, very intense," which is like saying nothing. Then he asks her to recite the poem a second and third time. Claudine is in some poetic happy-happy land, probably thinking if no one can understand the poem, it must be good.

Finally, the class and Caulfield give up. Rather than telling us the title, Claudine goes to her desk and very dramatically retrieves something from her backpack, hiding it until she's back in front of the class. She smiles broadly and lifts a glass ball over her head, shaking it. It's a snow globe.

"Excellent, Claudine," Caulfield says, asking her to recite the poem again, trying to make us account for every image, though even he can't make sense of the "boundaries of water," and for a good reason, because it doesn't make sense.

When it's Sara's and my turn, we have to walk past Claudine, who has a glow on, like she just got back from the beach, and I'd really like to upstage her with our poem.

Sara and I get situated, and she still looks very unhappy.

"Finally, a boy carrying the torch for us males," Caulfield says.

"Whatever," I almost say, then begin:

"The last automobile of night passes. Grandpa and I
crawl on a blanket of grass, surrounded by silence, except
for opening and closing of tiny dark doors. Flashlight in
my right hand, creatures scatter under its enormous eye,
or my grandpa grabs them, half out of holes, or damp
noses breaking the surface. Strange creatures, soft-bellied

fragments. My grandpa and I, two buddies to the end,
reach for a handful of them."

"A true guy poem," Caulfield says, "especially if you've ever gone fishing. Am I correct in guessing the title is 'Night Crawler'?"

Darn, I think, and tell him him he's right.

"Will you read it one more time?" And I do. Then he asks to look at my copy, and much to my amazement, he becomes ecstatic over the metaphors, asking the class what the "tiny dark doors" are and to explain how a flashlight can have an eye. I interrupt to say that all the good images are Sara's and that I focused mostly on the memory of my grandfather. This confession seems to be winning over Sara until Caulfield's eyes widen. What he says next ends up being very bad for me. In fact, it would've been better if he had pushed me off a bridge with an unattached bungee cord.

"Is this a prose poem, Benny?" he asks.

I start dancing. "Actually, there's a version with line breaks, but I forgot to bring it."

"No need, Mr. Wordsmith, because this wonderful poem proves that paragraphs and poetry aren't enemies. But that's not why I'm giving it a prize. Sara's imagery brings the power, but the poem also tells a story about a

grandfather and grandson. Your two sensibilities comple-
ment each other nicely."

I look at Sara, who leans over and whispers one word,
"Anonymous," then adds, "That was my whole point,
Benny, and you left it out. I think it's sweet you love your
grandpa, but we made a deal, and you know I didn't want
the poem to be a paragraph." Finished, she exchanges
glances with Claudine, who's looking at me as if I had just
kicked Hobo around the block.

Before I can explain myself, tears begin to spot Sara's
cheeks, and I finally get how big a deal this is for her.

Caulfield misunderstands the cause of Sara's tears and
says, "This is what good poetry can do." He reaches inside
his sports coat and retrieves a clean handkerchief, which he
offers to Sara, but she wants no part of it.

"Benny Alvarez," I hear. I'm expecting to see my
mother, but it's Claudine's voice.

Ms. D and Caulfield realize something strange is going
on and ask for an explanation, which Claudine, speaking
for Sara and every girl in class, is more than happy to pro-
vide. She says I didn't send Sara the final version, and that
the girls don't think prose poetry is poetry anyway.

"You think we believe Bob wrote any of your poem?"
I counter, and I'm not surprised to see every guy in the
classroom nodding, though it's clear this discussion isn't

about poetry anymore. Most of the guys couldn't care less about poetry. But I'm sure they remember the past classes when the girls took over and treated us like a bunch of morons.

"It might be best for me and Mr. Jones to step outside for a minute," Ms. D says, obviously wanting to find a solution to this conflict.

To be honest, I'm not too crazy about them leaving right now. I'm wondering if when they get back, I'll be huddled in a corner, tied up, beaten, and gagged. I look around the room, and everyone seems kind of confused. Fortunately, it doesn't take long for Ms. D and Caulfield to return.

"First of all," Ms. D says, "Mr. Jones and I don't think any prizes should be given. Everyone's poem is so good that we don't want to exclude anyone. Second, we have a question. Are we correct in thinking that most of the girls believe poetry can only be in verse and should rhyme, and that most of the boys think it doesn't matter?" She forgets the other alternative, that most of the boys don't care.

No one says anything, until Beanie blurts out, "What does it matter? Did anyone think Benny and Sara's poem was a prose poem when he read it?"

"If you've ever read any poetry," Paige says, "you'd know

it's been written with line breaks for thousands of years."

And then the unlikeliest of voices butts in. "So what?" Big Joe says. "We don't live a thousand years ago."

We argue back and forth like this for a few minutes until Caulfield interrupts everyone. "Ms. Butterfield and I have decided to turn this into a learning experience. How would you feel about a real contest, where one boy writes a prose poem and one girl writes a verse poem, and then the class can decide which one is best?"

"Only if Benny writes the prose poem," Beanie says, and all the guys agree.

"And only if Claudine writes the verse poem," Paige says, and all the girls nod their heads as one.

This is about the closest I've come to being class president, but somehow it doesn't feel so good.

"Can we agree on this, Claudine and Benny?" Ms. D asks.

"You bet," Claudine says.

I'm trying to respond, but Benny the Wordsmith is suddenly struck dumb.

"Benny?" Ms. D asks again, and Big Joe says, "He'll do it," so I agree.

"Ms. Butterfield and I," Caulfield adds, "have decided that you'll have a week to write a poem about love or loss."

Ms. D starts to explain what that means when the bell

rings, and five minutes later I find myself with Jocko and Beanie.

"All the guys will be counting on you, Benny," Beanie says.

"How can anyone in their right mind expect me to write a better poem than Claudine?"

"It doesn't matter," Beanie says. "Your poem can stink as long as it's not broken up or rhymes. And it won't stink because it will be a guy poem."

"He's right, dude," Jocko says, "but you really got yourself into it, didn't you? It's going to be a very weird party this weekend."

"What do you mean?"

Jocko points to the outdoor basketball courts, where Claudine and a bunch of girls are standing. They're staring at us and don't look very happy.

"The good news, Benny, is there's no reason to worry about dancing unless you want to dance with me."

LOVE OR LOSS

"Love or loss?" Irene says. She's sitting next to Aldo at the granite table. They're drinking Cokes and eating popcorn she just made. Crash and my grandfather are outside on the back porch, playing a board game. I guess all defenseless animals have been made safe, at least for now. The weather is growing cooler, so my grandfather has a red plaid shawl draped over his shoulders.

"Love or loss?" Aldo says, echoing Irene. "I mean, you haven't even started dating." In between eating, he's drumming on the table with two fingers to music only he can hear.

"Ms. Butterfield said to think of love in broad terms, like anything important to us. The same goes for loss."

"So you could write a poem about losing your favorite pencil?" Aldo asks.

"That's not funny," Irene says.

"No, Aldo's right," I say. "According to Caulfield Thomas Jones, you can write a poem on anything."

"I agree," Aldo says, "but this will teach you that girls take poetry very seriously."

"Anything else I should know?"

"Yeah, girls also expect you to think exactly like them. They're merciless."

Irene punches Aldo in the arm.

"Jocko already found that out. Becky Walters won't even talk to him until this contest is over."

"That's going to make for an interesting party," Irene says. "You really do have a way of creating drama, Benny."

"Is the dude mad at you?" Aldo asks.

"No, Jocko always has my back."

Aldo laughs. "Don't be so sure about that when it comes to girls."

As we're talking, Crash helps my grandfather through the sliding glass door leading from the porch to the sitting room. Sometimes I'm amazed at how fragile my grandfather is. It was only two years ago he was crushing golf balls on the range instead of putting them on the practice green.

"Who won, Grandpa?" I ask.

"Won what?"

"The game."

"We don't play to win, right, Crash?" At least he's got the name right today.

"Crash always plays to win, Grandpa."

"Grandpa and me have different rules," Crash says.

"Hey, Crash," Aldo says. "Benny's having girl trouble. Does that ever happen to you?"

Crash leads my grandfather to the recliner, and Aldo goes over to help.

"Any girls making your life miserable, Crash?"

"How could they do that?" Crash says.

"Well then, any hot girls in your class?"

"Hot?" Crash says.

"Yeah, you know what I mean?" But it's clear Crash doesn't think of girls like that.

"There's one girl," he says, "who's allergic to peanuts."

Grandpa starts laughing. "You gotta love this kid." Then he adds, "What girl troubles do you have, Benny? I'm an au . . . ," and he's struggling again for a word until Aldo offers "authority." "Yeah, I'm an authority on women. On which ones not to pick."

"Inappropriate, Grandpa," Irene says.

I tell Grandpa about Claudine and the contest, and about the topic of love and loss.

"Why don't you write a poem on Spot?" Crash says seriously, and on hearing his name, Spot stumbles toward us.

"I don't think so, Crash," I say, and everyone agrees.

"It'll come to you, Benny," my grandfather says. "You're an Alvarez; you'll find something horrible to write about. That's what I remember about poetry, a lot of sadness and anger and wars."

"It's different now, Grandpa; you can write about anything, even happy stuff."

"Who'd want to read that?"

"He's right," Aldo says. "Poetry should be about the human condition, and the human condition is pretty rugged."

I'm not sure what he means by the "human condition," but Irene knows because she says, "You have to stop hanging around with the Alvarez guys. You're starting to sound like them."

As she's talking, I notice my grandfather mumbling to himself. He's gaping at the sliding glass door, like he sees something the rest of us can't.

"What is it, Grandpa?"

"What's what?"

"What're you looking at?"

He doesn't answer, so I go to the window just in

time to see a hawk flying away from the house toward a wooded area. When I look back at my grandfather, he seems angry.

"What was it?" Crash asks.

"Just an airplane," I say.

A SICK DOG

The next morning Beanie shows up alone. "Jocko left before I got there."

"That's a first."

"Kind of serendipitous."

"Unexpected?"

"No."

"Tragic?"

"Wrong again."

"So what is it?"

"To be honest, I forgot."

"Not much of a game, Beanie, if you can't remember the word's meaning."

Instead of reaching for the Book, he says, "It'll come by lunch. That's the way my brain works. Like there's all this information banging around in there, and every once in a while, something comes into focus."

About twenty minutes later, we're walking toward the school's entrance when we see Jocko arguing with Becky Walters, though it looks like *she's* arguing and *he's* listening. She shakes her finger at him and walks away. When he sees us coming, he looks uncomfortable.

"Don't say anything," he says.

"Not a problem," I say.

But then he decides to clue us in. "She said if she had her way, she'd 'uninvite'—that was her word—every guy to her party."

"Did you tell her she meant 'disinvite'?" Beanie says.

Jocko shakes his head. "No, dude, I guess I forgot that important point."

"I'm sorry, Jocko," I say. "I feel like I messed you up."

"It's not your fault. They're taking this stuff too seriously, though you're the guy they'd like to spray to death with perfume. They think you're out to get Claudine, and they can't believe you're doing it while Hobo is dying."

"Hobo's dying? How was I supposed to know that?"

"He got worse a day ago."

"What am I, clairvoyant?"

"It's just a matter of days," Jocko says, "or at least that's Becky's take on it."

"You think she's telling the truth?"

"Of course she's telling the truth. It's not like she's a whack job." I start thinking about Aldo's warning and decide not to criticize Becky for fear of losing Jocko to the Dark Side.

"Well, I didn't have anything to do with Hobo dying," I say.

"No, you didn't," Jocko says. "Just bad timing."

Then we trudge off to homeroom.

In Mr. Congo's class we're laboring on algebra worksheets. I'm having trouble focusing on all the $5 + y$'s and $14 - y$'s because I keep staring at Claudine. I try to imagine what it would be like if Spot had cancer. He smells to high heaven, but he's almost as old as me. I don't have a memory that doesn't include him.

Claudine's working feverishly on our algebra problems until she senses my preoccupation with her. She looks up and makes this strange face, her eyes bulging, her head wobbling like one of those bobblehead dolls. It's a face that says, "What are you looking at, you nitwit?"

After class, she corners me and Beanie in the hall. "It's impolite to stare."

"I wasn't staring," I say, which is of course a lie.

"Yes, you were. Sometimes you're very creepy, like a bug."

Ouch. "I was just thinking about Hobo. I heard he was sick. I have a dog too."

"I don't need you to worry about Hobo, Benny Alvarez."

"There's no reason to be nasty," Beanie says. "He was just trying to be beneficent."

"That's not even the right word, Beanie. You guys think you're smart, but a monkey can look up words in a thesaurus."

I'm getting a little angry now. "I don't think that's true."

Her eyes are doing that crazy changing-color thing again, and as much as I'd like to yell at her, I can't. It's weird, but when she's angry, she seems more interesting to me.

"Just forget it, Beanie," I say.

On the way to Ms. D's class, I'm getting a lot of high fives from other seventh-grade guys. "You the man, Benny," one kid says. "Poetry sucks," says another dude, who usually says just about everything sucks. Just my luck that when I finally become a celebrity, some of my fans end up being morons.

Ms. D's class is uneventful until the very end, when she drops a bombshell on us.

"I have something to tell you," she says. Her hands are in front of her, palm to palm. Then she's interlocking her fingers, though swiftly changing her mind and rubbing her palms together again. It's like she can't decide whether she wants to make dough or pray.

"I know how quickly rumors travel in a small school, so I want you to know that I'm engaged to be married." At this announcement, all the girls let out a collective sigh, and Ms. D adds, "And my fiancé is Mr. Jones."

I'm not sure how I feel about this development, but in an instant, something very weird happens. Ms. D morphs before my eyes back to Ms. Butterfield. Although that Ms. D smile is more glorious than ever, she doesn't seem very intriguing anymore.

Later, Beanie's paging through the Book, reciting possible descriptions for the new Ms. D: "humdrum, dismal, drab, dreary," which seem like words to describe the weather. "Monotonous, uninteresting, and a word none of us can say that's spelled j-e-j-u-n-e." Then finally, Beanie comes upon "lackluster."

"Stop," I say. "What's the definition of that?"

"'Lacking brilliance or radiance or vitality and enthusiasm.'"

"From what you guys say, Ms. D certainly doesn't lack vitality or enthusiasm," Jocko says.

"It's still the right word," I argue. "We decided to call her Ms. Demigoddess because she was like those goddesses who appear in the movies, surrounded by glowing light. Somehow the picture of her trailing old stuffy Caulfield around for the rest of her life takes the shine off."

"I thought you liked the guy," Jocko says.

"I never went that far."

"Benny's right," Beanie says. "She lacks luster. As of today, I proclaim that Ms. D will forever be spoken of as Ms. Butterfield." Then he holds out his hand and Jocko places his on top of Beanie's, both of them waiting for me to do the same.

"Don't you think we ought to wait a few weeks?" I say. "Maybe the whole engagement will fall through."

"Then we'll go back to Ms. D," Jocko says.

"Can we do that?"

"Jeez, Benny," Beanie says, "it was your idea," so I place my hand on theirs and we say in one voice, "Agreed."

CRASH CRASHES

By Wednesday, I still don't have a topic for my poem. I'm nervous about that and also Becky Walters's party. But Wednesday is a good day, because I take my after-school class on how to draw cartoons. I'm probably the worst artist in the entire middle school, but Mrs. Jameson has no qualms about lying to me. She retired years ago and is one of the nicest people I know. Her hair, which is thin and mostly gone, is dyed a shoe-polish kind of brown, and she has bags under her eyes that nearly reach her cheekbones.

Today we're working on a still life. We were told to bring three objects from home and position them as we see fit. They should be objects that mean something to us. I brought one of Spot's plastic bones, a garage remote

control (don't ask me why), and a rabbit's foot my grandfather gave me. I position them on top of one another like
logs on a fire, then draw until Mrs. Jameson stops by. My
bone looks like an amoeba; my rabbit's foot, a bird's claw;
and the garage opener, a bologna sandwich.

"Pretty bad, huh?"

"Don't be so critical, Benny," Ms. Jameson says. "You're
improving every week. Why did you arrange them as you
have?"

"To me, it's like putting logs in the woodstove at home.
If you pile them the right way, you have a better fire."

"What a wonderful metaphor," she says, then adds
what she always does: "Whatever you lack in talent, and
that will change, you make up for with heart."

So much for Mr. Negativity.

"Thanks, Mrs. Jameson," I say.

She's about to offer some suggestions when we spot my
mother at the door, even though she's not supposed to pick
me up for another half hour. She looks flustered and gestures to Mrs. Jameson. They speak for a few minutes, then
Mrs. Jameson says I have to leave.

"Am I in trouble?"

"Of course not."

I pack up, and the first thing I ask my mother is, "Is
Dad dead?"

"Dad?"

"Well, he's always talking about dying."

"No, it's your grandfather."

"He's dead?"

"No, he's had another stroke. He had a seizure, too, so we're not sure how severe it will be."

"Where's Dad?"

"He had to go to Boston to interview someone for his book, and there's a huge accident on the interstate, so it may be hours before he gets home."

"Does Crash know?"

"Yes, and that's the problem. We don't know where he is. I'll explain in the car."

It's pouring outside, so we run to our minivan. Inside, my mother says that when my father phoned her about the stroke and said he was stuck in traffic, she left work to be home for Crash, but he wasn't there. On the answering machine was an earlier frantic message from Gloria, who finished by saying, "I think this is the end."

"And Crash played it when he got home?"

"Yes."

"Why didn't Gloria call Dad on his cell?"

"Maybe she was overwhelmed at the time."

"So no one knows where Crash is? Jeez, it's raining pretty hard."

"I know."

"Did you call Irene? You know how Crash feels about Aldo."

"They're at the house waiting for us."

When we get there, Crash is still AWOL. My mother's about to call the police when the phone rings.

"Benny?" It's my father.

"Yeah?"

"I just got a call from Bob Nicholson."

"At Firefly?"

"Yeah, he says Crash is there. He's putting on the practice green."

"It's pouring."

"Bob tried to coax him inside, but he won't go. He even threatened Bob with his putter."

I can almost hear Grandpa saying, "You gotta love that kid."

"How did he get there? It's about five miles away."

"Don't know, but you and Aldo should pick him up, and I'll call when I get to the hospital."

"Sorry about Grandpa," I say.

"Don't worry. He's a tough guy."

When I hang up, Aldo and I drive to Firefly. We pull into the parking lot, which is empty except for one car. It's still raining fairly hard, and I can see a small figure tossing a coin behind his back, then putting. Mr. Nicholson comes out of the clubhouse, holding an umbrella over his head. "I tried to talk him inside, but he's really stubborn."

"We know," I say.

When Mr. Nicholson trots away, I tell Aldo I'll handle this one myself, and he offers me Irene's umbrella, but I refuse, saying, "Crash would want me to get wet with him."

Aldo laughs, then stops. "Sorry, it really isn't funny."

"That's okay. Grandpa would appreciate the humor."

"You're right."

When I walk toward the green, Crash pretends he doesn't see me, so I stand quietly, watching him go through my grandfather's ritual.

"Grandpa's not going to die," I finally say.

"You don't care anyway." He faces me, and I'm pretty sure he's crying, but it's hard to tell with the rain.

"That's not fair, Crash."

"After the last stroke, you and Dad said he'd be better off dead. You guys talk around me like I'm not there."

"We didn't say that, Crash. I said I wouldn't want Grandpa to live if he's a vegetable."

"But he isn't. Mom's right—you're just negative."

"How did you get here?"

"I walked, then some woman gave me a ride."

"Some woman?"

"Yeah, she felt bad because I was getting wet."

I feel like smacking him for getting in a stranger's car. "Let's just tell Dad you walked here, okay?"

"Okay," he says. "Is Grandpa really going to live? Gloria doesn't think so."

"We don't know much yet, but no one's talking about him dying."

"Gloria did."

"Sometimes Gloria gets hysterical. Do you mind if I play with you?"

"You don't have your putter."

"I can use yours."

"Mine's too short."

"Come on, Crash, help me out here."

And so we putt around for a while, the golf ball struggling to roll over the wet green. The rain continues to pound us, my hoodie and jeans sticking to my skin. I feel very tired and drained, and even a bit sad, but I try to be strong for Crash. After about ten minutes of putting, Crash says matter-of-factly, "We can go home now," so we trudge back to Aldo's car.

"We're going to mess up your seats," I say to Aldo.

"Don't worry about it. They're leather."

"Hi, Aldo," Crash says, like nothing important has

happened over the last two hours.

"You scared the heck out of us," Aldo says.

"I guess that's why they named me Crash."

Later that night, we learn my grandfather will recover, though he has to stay in the hospital for now. We're told he'll be very weak and may have to use a cane or wheelchair for a while.

I'm about to fall asleep when my father comes into my room. He looks tired, removing his glasses and rubbing his eyes. "You okay?" he asks.

"I guess."

"In the future, we have to watch what we say around Crash."

"You mean about Grandpa dying."

"Yeah."

"But it's what we felt."

"I'm not blaming you, Benny. I'm one of the great blowhards of all time, but there's a difference between being brutally honest and being insensitive." He's about to leave when he asks, "Did you write your poem yet?"

"No, but I want it to be be on Grandpa."

"Won't that be tough now?"

"I dunno."

"You ever think of choosing a good memory, like you

did in that night crawler poem? I'm sure that would perk him up."

"I'll think about it," I say.

After my father leaves, I clutch the rabbit's foot I brought to art class. Unlike any Alvarez I've heard of, my grandfather used to hunt, and my father says smoked venison used to hang in their attic. Before his strokes, my grandfather also tinkered with wood, and my room is scattered with birds he crafted and painted.

Thinking about this, I go to my desk and write these two sentences: "Grandpa cocking his hunting rifle. Something to sink one's teeth into, like smoked deer meat hanging in the attic."

AN EXTRAORDINARY EVENT

The next day at school everyone is more excited about the poetry contest than I am. Some kids tape posters to the hallways without asking, and they're immediately torn down. Too bad, because some of them are funny, my favorite showing a kid writing a series of paragraphs with "Poetry don't need no line breaks" scribbled at the bottom in red Magic Marker.

Even some of the eighth graders have taken an interest, though most of them act like we're all stupid little kids. After all, they're going to high school next year. Big deal, dudes.

"You certainly have polarized the seventh grade," Jocko says right before school starts.

"Polarized" should be an easy one, but Beanie and I can't wrap our minds around it.

"I mean we've got two factions butting heads because of you."

Now we're confused. Is "polarized" or "faction" the word of the day, or is he looking for us to guess the origins of "butting heads"?

"Take your pick," Jocko says, and so Beanie and I go to work. I'm enjoying the wordplay. It gets my mind off the contest and also distracts me from the hate looks I'm getting from girls, though something extraordinary—you might even say uplifting—happens at recess.

I start to obsess about my grandfather again, wandering off by myself to a picnic table near a jungle gym. I sit down and contemplate a few huge whitish-gray clouds frozen in the sky. Supposedly, my grandfather is improving, though he's having trouble swallowing, so the doctors have temporarily inserted a tube down his throat. I kind of hate them for doing that, and I'm not allowed to see him yet, so all I can do is imagine his anger. I feel like punching someone or crying, but there isn't anyone I dislike enough to punch, and since the stroke, I haven't been able to cry once, even though I often feel like it.

There's a noise to my left made by a few small birds pecking around the base of a tree. I reach into my pocket, removing a plastic bag of oyster crackers I'm saving for a snack. I crumble up a few of the crackers and toss them to the birds, teasing them closer with each throw. I'm just about done when a familiar voice says my name, but this time quietly. I turn to find Claudine standing about three feet away. Her hair is tied back, which always makes her face seem full and her eyes larger. When the sun breaks through a cloud, the blue-green surfaces of her irises reflect the rays, making them shimmer. She seems serene or, like me, maybe just tired. I brace myself for the inevitable insult, or perhaps she's decided to stab me with a bowie knife she no doubt has concealed inside her knee-high boots.

"Benny?" she says.

Before I can respond, she adds, "I'm sorry about your grandfather. I hope he gets better." She doesn't smile or try to touch me, but instead does an about-face and jogs toward her friends.

After she's gone, Jocko and Beanie join me.

"What nasty thing did she say now?" Beanie says. "You'd think she'd lay off until Monday."

"She said she hopes my grandpa gets better."

"I told Becky what happened," Jocko says. "Sorry, I should've asked if that was okay."

"It's probably a trick," Beanie says.

I'm thinking he's wrong this time, though I'm not sure why, and I decide to drop the conversation and be happy just to get through the day, dodging as many Benny haters as possible.

After dismissal, Beanie goes off to visit his grandpa, and a half hour later, I find myself playing Ping-Pong with Jocko in his basement. The basement itself is unfinished and unheated, and because there's no rug on the floor, it's a bit chilly. Although Jocko's never beaten me in Ping-Pong, he's whipping me today with overhand smashes.

"You letting me win, Benny?" he asks. "I'd really hate that."

He's right. I sometimes take pity on him and make it close.

"No, I'm playing my best."

"You don't look so good."

And he's right again. I've had a tickle in my throat since I got up, and my stomach feels like something's gone rotten in it.

"Is this poetry contest getting to you?"

"A little. I'm worried about my grandpa, too, and I think I got a cold from putting with Crash in the wet rain."

"You written the poem yet?"

"Nope."

155

"We're counting on you."

"Well, you shouldn't. If I'm a huge success, your girl-friend won't like you very much."

"I wouldn't say she's my girlfriend."

This conversation is feeling weird now.

"It's not like I'm accusing you of cruelty to animals, dude."

Jocko laughs. "Strange comparison." Then he changes the subject. "Becky told me Hobo's making a recovery. That dog doesn't want to die."

Who does? I think, picturing my grandfather hooked up like Frankenstein's monster to tubes and electrodes.

FEVER

At night I'm feeling worse. My stomach's unsettled and my throat's stinging, like someone slit my tonsils with a razor. But I don't complain because my parents are already stressed, sometimes ending their conversations in midstream when I enter a room. Crash and I want to go to the hospital, but my grandfather's still in intensive care, so we have to wait.

At about two a.m., I'm awakened by a series of bad dreams, each one ending with my grandfather sitting in a wheelchair, the plaid shawl around his shoulders, waving good-bye. My sheets are soaked in sweat, so I'm hoping my fever has broken. I go to my desk and look at the first line of my poem, whispering it over and over until it feels like a chant. Then other images come, and an hour later I end up with a first draft. I'm so tired I don't even reread it, just fall onto the bed into a deep sleep.

I wake in the morning, surprised to discover I'm not much better. I'm not nauseous, but my throat still burns, and my left ear's sore, like someone's jabbing a sharp object into it. I should stay home, but my mother has an important meeting, and my father needs to be with my grandfather, so I lie, telling them I'm okay. To make matters worse, it's raining, and before long, I find myself walking to school with Beanie and Jocko, shivering and holding a little black umbrella over my head. They're talking about the contest, and about Becky's party, and about the Patriots, and then Beanie uses the word "blewit" in a sentence, like we can ever guess that one. I'm only half hearing what they say, my brain numbed by fever.

"Have you finished the poem?" Beanie asks.

I've been asked that by so many guys over the last few days that it's nice to tell them I have, and I explain how I wrote the poem the previous night.

"Boy, Caulfield would love that story," Beanie says.

"Why?" Jocko asks.

"He freaks over that hocus-pocus stuff—you know, the whole thing about poets getting divine inspiration."

158

"Does that mean we have to call you Mr. Demigod now, Benny?"

"How about Mr. Burned-Out?" I say.

"You do look bad," Beanie says.

There's got to be a better word for how lousy I feel, so I retrieve the Book from my back pocket. "Frightful, ghastly, gruesome, monstrous, crappy . . ."

"I vote for all of them," Jocko jokes.

"Agreed," Beanie says.

"Thanks, dudes. I feel so much better now."

I make it through classes, ignoring all the Benny lovers and Benny haters. At lunch I'm confronted with a ham-and-cheese sandwich, which, right now, is about as appealing as mouse stew. Excuse the reference, Hector. I'm in a fog, glancing from table to table, everyone seeming to move in slow motion. Beanie sits next to me and doesn't look very happy. Jocko joins us and looks worse.

"What happened now?" I ask.

"Hobo died," Jocko says.

"Really?"

"Of course really, dude. Becky just told me."

"I thought he was getting better."

"I guess he didn't."

I understand why they feel bad. For years, we've seen

that dog follow Claudine to school each morning, then stand guard at dismissal. He's as much a part of our routine as the pizza the cafeteria serves every Friday.

"Becky says Claudine is hurting, so you should be nice to her, Benny."

I'm pretty fed up at this point.

"Give me a break, Jocko," I say. "I'm sick, my grandfather might be dying, I have to recite a poem at least half the class has already decided to hate, and by the way, I don't go out of my way to make Claudine feel lousy. I'm sad her dog died. Just last week I told her I was sorry he was sick, and she yelled at me."

"He's right," Beanie says.

"But not about busting Claudine," Jocko says.

"I'm outta here," I say, closing my lunch box and leaving the cafeteria, stopping at the bathroom to puke, and eventually ending up in front of an ancient nurse, who makes me suck on a thermometer. It doesn't take long for her to call my mother, who comes shortly afterward to pick me up.

When she arrives, I apologize, telling her I know she has enough on her mind.

"Don't be silly. I canceled my meeting."

"Won't you get in trouble?"

"Not if I don't pay attention to trouble."

I'm not sure what that means, but I assume it's positive.

CHICKEN SOUP FOR THE TROUBLED TEEN

When we get home, Spot's at the front door, barking, every little yelp echoing in my head like thunder. He quiets down when he recognizes me, rubbing his butt against my leg. I pet him before going to my room, where I fall on my bed, not waking until about four o'clock. I'm still feverish and my eyelids are caked shut, so I go to the bathroom and throw water on my face. Back in my room, I lie in bed, staring at a wall poster of Dustin Pedroia, who's looking a lot happier than me. There's a knock on my door, and before I can say "Come in," Crash appears, cupping a steaming bowl in his hands, while pinching a book under his right armpit.

"Irene made you chicken soup," he says. "She's baking bread, too."

When he hands me the bowl, the book falls to the floor. Before retrieving it, he pulls a spoon from his back pocket.

"Hope you weren't farting on the way here," I say. "That's a dangerous place to put a spoon."

He takes me seriously and says, "I only do that after breakfast, or when I have too many grapes."

"What's the book?"

"Mom bought it for you." He fetches it from the floor and hands it to me.

I read the title out loud: "*Chicken Soup for the Troubled Teen.*"

"What does that mean?"

"Looks like Mom's trying to convert me while I'm vulnerable." I scan the back cover, which gives a more in-depth description.

It's not easy being a teenager, but this book will help you to deal with all the triumphs and disappointments you'll have to face. The real-life experiences in this book act as a guide on topics such as first love, bullies, friendships, and most important, how to understand your parents' concerns, so you're all learning from each other, instead of arguing. So hold on tight; this trip won't always be

smooth, but you'll soon find out that no matter what
your problems are, you're not alone.

"I'm not too crazy about the 'troubled teen' reference,"
I say.

"Yeah, it's kind of insulting."

"You think I'm capable of mastering all this stuff,
Crash?"

"Not really?"

"Well, I guess I'll have to read it to find out."

"It would sure make Mom happy."

"Then it's worth a read, don't you think?"

He smirks, thinking I'm making fun of him.

"I hope they don't have chicken soup books for me,"
he says.

"Why? Don't you want to understand Mom and Dad?"

"Not if I have to walk around with a phony smile."

I set the book on my nightstand. "Right now, I'm more
interested in real chicken soup. Why don't you grab a bowl
for yourself and see if that bread's done? Tell Irene I promise to be nice to Aldo for at least a month."

Crash smiles. "Aldo's cool. Even Dad's liking him."

"What makes you say that?"

"He doesn't call him a Neanderthal anymore."

"Yeah, I guess the true sign of an Alvarez liking you is

when he doesn't insult you."

"But he still hates Rhode Island drivers."

That one makes me laugh, which isn't much fun when you have a sore throat.

"Just get some soup, okay?" I say.

About fifteen minutes later, Crash reappears with his soup and some freshly baked bread, and this time he has the phone under his armpit. He places the bread on my nightstand, then hands me the phone.

"What's this for?"

"Dad said we can call Grandpa. He said not to expect too much."

"He's getting better?"

"Dad said he'll explain later."

Crash hands me a sheet of paper with a phone number and extension on it. I wait for my grandfather to answer, but Gloria picks up.

"It's Benny," I say.

"Oh, Benny, I've had a time of it." Gloria has a tendency to focus on herself.

"Can Grandpa talk?"

"I'll ask him."

A few seconds later, I hear my grandfather's voice. He's having trouble pronouncing my name, so Gloria says, "It's Benny, your grandson."

"Hi, honey," he says, and that's the first time he's ever called me that.

"You okay, Grandpa?"

"Trouble swallowing. Just so tired. We'll get that hawk, don't you worry."

"It's Benny, Grandpa. Crash and I wanted to say we need you back for our Alvarez putting contest."

Meanwhile, Crash is trying to grab the phone from my hand. "Here, Grandpa," I say. "Crash wants to talk to you."

Crash takes the phone, and because he's nervous, he chatters, which is probably good since I don't expect my grandfather to make much sense. When the call ends, Crash says, "I didn't understand what he was talking about."

"He'll get better. After every stroke, it's like his head's littered with parts of a jigsaw puzzle, and he has to piece them together."

"It still stinks."

I hand him his soup. "Yeah, but maybe a little chicken soup will cheer us up."

"You sound like Mom."

"I'll take that as a compliment."

"It isn't."

After Crash leaves, my mother stops by with a thermometer. Then she wants to talk about the book. "I'm

165

not forcing it on you," she says. "Just read it when you're ready."

"Maybe it's better to wait until I'm twenty—then I can look back at my teen years and see all the good times I missed."

"Benny Alvarez," my mother says, smiling.

Next, my sister visits, bearing the gift of more bread. She wants to know how the girls at school are treating me and if she can read my poem.

"I'm going to rewrite it tonight."

"Shouldn't you sleep?"

"Actually, this fever makes me feel more creative."

"Well, at least you don't have to worry about the party tomorrow."

I had almost forgotten.

"Mom won't let you go now."

I should be happy, but I think about Jocko and Beanie there, and it doesn't seem right. Also, I wonder if Claudine will show, and if she's okay.

"Maybe I'll feel better tomorrow," I say.

"You should look in the mirror, dude." I can tell she's enjoying saying the word "dude."

She's not gone for more than two minutes when my father knocks.

"What is this, tag-team wrestling?" I say.

"You're just loved and honored in the Alvarez household, Benny."

"I'm not dying, am I, and everyone's paying their last respects?"

"No, that will happen on Monday when you read your poem."

"Not funny, Dad."

"Actually, I'm not feeling too great." As he talks, he keeps rubbing the back of his neck.

"How bad is Grandpa?"

"Hard to say. I feel like he's aware of everything, but for every sentence that makes sense, four don't. The doctors seem more worried about the swallowing, so he has to get that back before they'll let him go. Still, they say he may be home in a few days."

"I really feel bad for him," I say.

My father looks at me and grimaces. "Today I wondered again about his quality of life, but then I showed him pictures of you all, and he perked up, especially when he saw you and him putting and Crash holding his Nerf gun, about to take down a few aliens."

I laugh.

"We'll just have to see what happens." Then he places the palm of his hand on my forehead. "You feeling better?"

"Not much."

"Get some sleep. If you don't improve tomorrow, I'll take you to a walk-in clinic. It's the only place open on Saturday."

When he leaves, I work on my poem for a while, reading and rereading it, hoping to make it better. I began the poem thinking of beating Claudine, but now she and everyone else don't matter. My grandfather is my audience. I want to read it to him. I want to see him smile and hear him say, "You gotta love this kid," and this time the "kid" will be me.

PARTY POOPER

By two p.m. on Saturday, I've thrown up again and spent two hours at the walk-in clinic, where my father complains to the receptionist about the long wait. Then he informs twelve other hacking and shivering people that our health care system is equal to that of a number of Third World countries.

As it turns out, my tonsils are inflamed and I have an ear infection, so the doctor writes me a prescription for an antibiotic and tells me to rest for a few days.

"Will I be better by Monday?" I ask.

"Probably. Antibiotics work best when we give the body time to heal. But nowadays I can't get people to slow down."

"Tell me about it," my father says, happy to find a kindred soul.

When we return home, Aldo's in the sitting room with Irene.

"Wow, you look bad," he says.

"That's the general consensus."

Irene is searching the closet for her jacket but stops to ask how I am.

"I'll survive," I say.

"Best to stay away from Aldo," she says. "He has two gigs this weekend."

"Not to worry," Aldo says. "I have a strong immune system."

"Next you'll be telling us you're a vegan," my father says. He's cleaning the refrigerator, wearing yellow elbow-high rubber gloves, jeans, and an old gray T-shirt.

"Not to worry, Mr. Alvarez. Every self-respecting Cro-Magnon is a carnivore."

"The truth will reveal itself when I get the private investigator's report."

"Private investigator?"

"Yeah, the one I hired to follow you."

Aldo knows my father's joking but still seems taken aback.

"You're costing me a lot of money," my father adds,

scrubbing a rack that's stained with mustard and ketchup.

"And I was hoping you'd save it for Irene's dowry," Aldo says.

"Don't let my father scare you," Irene jokes, finally locating her jacket.

"Yeah, like he does my friends," I say.

"You mean Beanhead and Jerko?" my father says. "Actually, I like those guys."

"Well, they're terrified of you, and you're my dad, so I want them to like you."

"The day I need Beanbrain and Jacko as friends will be a sad day indeed, but tell them I think we should all go candlepin bowling next week. We can sit around, sip Dr Peppers, munch chips, and talk about Ms. D."

"Can I come?" Aldo pleads, trying to bust my father.

"That's Benny's decision."

Aldo looks longingly at me, so I change the subject. "Where are you going?"

"To see Grandpa," Irene says.

Everyone becomes more serious now.

"I didn't know we could visit him."

"That's because you can't," my father says. "The last thing he needs is a bad cold."

"Are Mom and Crash there?"

"No," Irene says. "Mom took Crash clothes shopping."

"May she rest in peace," my father says. Everyone is laughing except me. I just want to go upstairs, grab a graphic novel, and nod off. Which is what I decide to do.

About four p.m. I wake to reddish sunlight flooding my bedroom and a cool wind rattling the windowpanes. I wonder what Beanie and Jocko bought Becky and whether they got dressed up, or if Big Joe was invited by accident, showing up wearing a dog collar and leash and tugged around Becky's backyard by Paige. I wonder what music they played and whether any of the boys danced with girls, and whether you had to eat differently at parties like these. I've seen Beanie make a slice of cake disappear in one gulp, and Jocko has a habit of constantly burping when he drinks soda and of wiping his greasy fingers on his pants.

I'm bored, so I tinker with my poem until I have it just right. Then I fall back to sleep, this time not waking until it's dark. My mother's standing over me like a ghost.

"Your friends are downstairs."

"Jocko and Beanie?"

"They came after the party ended. They brought you some cake and a party favor."

"But I didn't go."

"Becky's mother knows you're sick."

I'm hoping the party favor is an iPod, or a yo-yo, or maybe Becky burned a Bruno Mars CD. I sit up, feeling a little grungy. My fever seems to have broken with the last nap, so my clothes are damp and smell like sickness. "Will you tell them to wait a few minutes? I need to shower."

"Okay," she says.

After I clean up and change, I go downstairs, finding Beanie and Jocko in the sitting room, talking to Crash. They don't look much different than usual, except their shirts are tucked in.

"The walking dead," Jocko says.

"Boy, did we miss you," Beanie adds.

"Sorry you had to wait."

"Not to worry," Beanie says. "We were entertained by Crash complaining about clothes shopping."

Crash is wearing a new pair of cargo jeans and playing with one of my yo-yos. "Three hours, Benny," he says, "in and out of dressing rooms, arguing with Mom, all these teenage girls telling me I'm cute. What a bunch of liars!"

"Sounds good to me," Jocko says.

"Yeah, right," Crash says. "Even you guys couldn't find a word for that torture."

"Don't be so sure," Beanie says, and pulls out the Book. "Torture: affliction, agony, anguish, dolor, martyrdom, twinge . . ."

"Why do you guys waste your time with that junk?" He releases the yo-yo, doing the Walk the Dog trick, the yo-yo spinning on the floor away from him, then snapping back into his palm.

"Be careful what you say," Jocko says, giving Crash a playful headlock, then letting him go.

"Why mess around when all those words mean the same thing?" Crash says. Then he performs the Rock the Baby trick.

"Very impressive," Jocko says. "Keep practicing, so you'll be able to support yourself after you get out of high school and can't find a job."

"Huh?" Crash says.

"What Jocko means," I say, "is the difference between those words *is* important. If you're being tortured, you can call the cops on Mom. If shopping causes twinges of agony, then get over it. And if you think you're a martyr after trying on three pairs of pants, you're a whack job."

"Bravo, Benny," Beanie says.

"Very eloquent," Jocko adds.

Meanwhile Crash can't figure out if we're educating or making fun of him. "Dad's right about you guys," he says, then Walks the Dog again, this time following the imaginary creature into another room.

"What's that supposed to mean?" Jocko says. "I thought your father liked me."

"He doesn't like anyone," Beanie says.

"Not true," I say. "He just gets ticked off by stupidity. I can relate."

"As the Book says," Jocko reports, "the apple doesn't fall far from the tree."

I can't argue about that, so instead, I ask about the party. "Did they hang a Benny Alvarez piñata from a tree and pummel it with cheerleading batons?"

"Actually," Jocko says, "you've been temporarily forgiven for being Claudine's enemy, mostly because I told them about your grandfather."

"How's Claudine doing?"

"She didn't show."

"Really?"

"Yeah, really."

"So what did you all do?"

"It wasn't that bad," Beanie says "Some decent music, and the food was incredible. They had these things that look like hot dogs but are twice as fat and taste like steak. Amazing."

"Did you play games?"

"Just the usual," Jocko says. "Bobbing for apples and pin the tail on the donkey."

"You're kidding."

"Of course I'm kidding. It wasn't a big deal, dude. Some music, some food, then we all talked a little."

"And Jocko danced," Beanie says, smiling.

Jocko glares at him. "You did too."

"Beanie?"

"Yeah, he danced with Paige."

They might as well have told me they skydived with no parachute. "I didn't know you guys danced."

"We didn't either," Beanie says. "We kind of moved around, feeling the beat," and then he slips into a very strange dance, looking like he's dodging punches while getting kicked in the shins.

"Will you do me a favor, Beanie?"

He stops dancing. "Sure."

"Smack me in the face."

"What?"

"I'm having a very bad nightmare, and I'm afraid if I don't come out of it fast, you'll start slow dancing with Jocko and kiss him on the cheek."

Everyone laughs at that one. Then Beanie gives me a little red box with a yellow ribbon around it. "It's your party favor."

"What is it?"

"We don't want to ruin the surprise," Jocko says.

I open the box and inside, cushioned by cotton, is a gold pin in the shape of a butterfly. "This is it?"

"Yeah, it was the only weird moment of the party.

Becky's father handed them out, then talked about how Becky was their butterfly, describing all the stages a butterfly undergoes before"—and Beanie finishes the sentence—"'blossoming into a wonder of nature.'"

"He really said that?"

"Yeah."

"Did you laugh?"

"First," Jocko says, "I'm not sure it's something to laugh about. Second, Becky's father's a big cop, so if he told me to address her as Your Highness, I probably would. And finally, every girl at the party sighed at the same time when they saw that pin."

"Yeah," Beanie says. "It was very weird."

"And considering the big showdown on Monday," Jocko says, "I didn't want to tick off anyone, especially Becky."

"What did the guys do?"

"Most of them probably forgot about the pin when the cake arrived."

I hold the pin in my hand and wonder what party favor my parents would choose for me. Probably a whoopee cushion or joy buzzer.

At that thought, my mother suddenly appears with a bowl of chips. "I'll get some Cokes, but I want you to have ginger ale," she says to me.

We sit for a while drinking our sodas and eating chips. They mostly want to talk about my poem and if I'll be well enough to recite it. "The whole world's watching," Jocko says.

"Maybe she won't show," Beanie says, "and you win by default. Hobo bailed you out."

"What a jerky thing to say," Jocko protests.

"Jocko's right, Beanie. I wouldn't want to win like that."

"Well, I was just saying."

"Well, don't," I say.

When we're done talking, I play some dance music and say I'll pay them to show me their moves. "Nice try, Benny," Jocko says, before he and Beanie hustle out the front door.

As my mother cleans up, she asks me how I'm feeling.

"Better," I say.

"Have you finished your poem?"

"The question of the week. Yeah, I have."

"Can I read it?"

"I'd rather you not."

She gives me that hurt look mothers are so good at and says, "I wouldn't want to make you feel uncomfortable."

I have two choices. I can spend an hour discussing why I'm uncomfortable ("There's nothing wrong with showing feelings," "I want to know the inner Benny"), or I can let her read the poem, which is what I decide to do.

A few minutes later, she's sitting in the recliner, and I'm feeling a bit nervous. She positions her reading glasses on the bridge of her nose and scans the page. "So this is what's causing all the commotion?"

"Unfortunately, yes."

She nods, then reads quietly to herself. After a first pass, she goes back for a second, then something very strange happens. Her eyes well up and a few tears spot her cheeks. "This is beautiful. I wish your grandfather could read it."

"I plan to recite it to him."

"Will you do something for me, Benny?"

I figure it can't be any riskier than letting her read my poem. "Sure," I say.

"Realize that Monday there are no losers. Your poem already makes you a winner."

"But not in the real world."

"Yes, in the real world too."

"But not in the Alvarez world."

She mulls that over, then hands the poem back, kissing me on the cheek and going quietly upstairs.

Later, I lie in bed thinking about her crying, and I kind of envy her. The Alvarez boys have never been big on crying, so instead, I'm stuck with a numbing kind of sadness, as if something bad is lurking, like a bullet with "Benny Alvarez" etched on its casing, and I think of what my grandpa said: "Trouble can't hit a moving target."

Keep moving, Benny, I think. *Keep moving.*

SURPRISE, SURPRISE

By Sunday, I'm feeling better but decide to hang around the house, working on my poem and playing board games with Crash. Monday morning I'm strong enough for school, though still coughing up ugly green mucus. I fear, or maybe hope, that while I'm reading my poem I'll launch a huge loogie onto Big Joe's forehead. When I come down for breakfast, my mother and Irene have already gone. My father and Crash are eating cereal at the round granite table, wearing cardboard crowns from Burger King. They pretend not to see me.

"I say, old chap," my father says to Crash, "looking so forward to the troubadour's performance today."

"Aye, matey," Crash replies, mixing up time periods and characters.

"Very funny," I say.

"Ah, and herewith he comes," my father says, jumping off his chair and bowing to me. Not bad for an old guy.

I grab a big wooden spoon on the kitchen counter and tap him lightly on the shoulder. "I knight you Sir Alvarez the Negative."

He rises and removes his crown. "There's not a big leap from being negative to being funny, Benny. As Mark Twain said, 'Against the assault of laughter nothing can stand.'"

"Not even Claudine?"

He laughs and gives me a hug. "Pancakes or waffles? It's your day."

"Pancakes," I say.

"Can I have some too?" Crash asks.

"Sure thing, Your Majesty."

"Can I wear this crown to school?" Crash says. "I wanna prank Paulie." Paulie is Crash's best friend.

"Why not? Halloween's not far off."

While my father prepares pancakes, I ask about my grandfather.

"He's swallowing okay, and they said we can bring him home on Wednesday if things get better. He's taking some meds that make him very tired, though, so he slept about sixteen hours yesterday."

"Can he walk?" One of my grandfather's worst fears is being in a wheelchair.

"Yeah, but we'll have to help him for a while, and he has that cane he refuses to use."

Crash is finishing his cereal, not saying much of anything. That's how he's been dealing with the stroke, pretending it doesn't exist.

My father looks at him. "If he gets out on Wednesday, he wants to sit on the porch with Crash and watch the birds feed."

"Gloria okay with that?"

"She wants him to be happy, she says, 'in his last days.'"

"Why does she talk like that? She makes us guys look like optimists."

"Yeah, but she's always there for your grandpa. She's a trouper."

"It's going to be sunny and sixty degrees on Wednesday," Crash blurts out.

"Great day for bird-watching," I say, hoping I, too, can have one-on-one time with my grandfather that day, maybe read to him.

Crash still doesn't look up, nodding his head so vigorously, the Burger King crown nearly slides off.

My father decides to take us to school because I'm still a little weak. Fortunately, it seems all the psychotic Rhode Island drivers have their cars in for servicing today, so he doesn't have much to complain about. At school, Beanie and Jocko joke around, but I'm too uptight to join in. Instead, I give them copies of my poem, asking them not to read it until later.

Whether it's the medication or the contest, I'm feeling spaced out: not happy, not sad, just kind of dazed. Which is in contrast to everyone else, who seems wired. The high fives and Benny-hating stares begin the moment I enter school, though Becky Walters breaks free from her crew long enough to say she's sorry my grandfather's sick. Before math, I bump into Claudine once or twice, but she refuses to make eye contact. I want to tell her I'm sorry about Hobo but have trouble reading her face. She has to be sick from sadness if she missed both school and the party, but she's putting up a good front. She looks nice, nothing flashy or bright: a white, long-sleeved button-up sweater and blue dress slacks whose cuffs rest on navy leather sandals. I'm wearing jeans, a gray hoodie, and running shoes. Not a good start, I think, if the judges vote on appearance.

I make a point of facing forward in Mr. Congo's class, and on my way out the door, I'm surprised when he says, "Knock 'em dead, Benny."

"Thanks," I say, then peer into the hallway, happy to see Claudine isn't there. I imagined fighting my way through a mass of angry seventh-grade girls reciting sonnets and poking me with No. 2 pencils.

Ms. Butterfield and Caulfield Thomas Jones are sitting on the desk again, waiting for everyone to arrive. They're both very excited, not realizing that one contestant has lost her dog, and the other has a sick grandfather and a pound of snot packed in his nose.

"Let's settle down," she says. "Mr. Jones and I want to say a few things. First, I can't say how proud I am of how you've taken to poetry, whether it's verse poetry"—and she looks at Claudine—"or prose poetry," then she turns to me. "I'm hoping that by the end of class, we all agree that poetry can be found in everything: in the shell of a snail or a fallen tree, in cutting the lawn or cleaning a gutter. Poetry is not just written. It's lived. It gives us those small moments when, for even a brief second or two, we can feel immortal." At that last word, it appears that she's about to cry, until Caulfield places his hand on hers. "I'm just very proud of you all," she says.

When she finishes, everyone is quiet, realizing she means every word she said.

Caulfield's turn is next, and he does a very un-Caulfield kind of thing. He's usually king of one-liners, those snappy little phrases that suggest he's the wittiest guy this side of Mars. But rather than making a joke, he says he's brought doughnuts and juice, and that after the contest, we'll have a party.

"Cool," Big Joe says.

Then Caulfield clears out a section of the room, dragging over a podium he must have borrowed from the auditorium. "Ms. Butterfield and I have decided, in the spirit of courtly love poetry, that ladies shall go first." He bows ceremoniously for Claudine to come forward.

It seems to take her forever to get there. She rests her poem on the podium, slowly scanning the room. Then she focuses on me for a second, her chest making slight heaves.

The wait is killing me, but she's in no hurry to begin. It's clear this experience is very painful for her, and I can see her fighting back tears.

She takes another deep breath and says, "This is a poem for Hobo, my dog. He died last week."

Something very odd happens at this point. As I'm listening to her, my mind is flooded with a sea of unrelated images: my grandfather touching my hand, Crash and me sleeping on the pool table, my father yelling at a double-parked vehicle, Hobo waiting for Claudine outside school, Jocko and Beanie dancing, and on and on to the point where I'm having trouble breathing, and I see that Benny

Alvarez sadness bullet speeding toward me. I wish I could go for a run, or shoot a few baskets, anything to dodge it, so I try to focus on Claudine. I've never seen her so shaky, but she gathers herself and says very slowly, "Hobo: A Verse Poem in Three Stanzas."

When she finishes, at first there's dead silence, and I can't decide if I'm more impressed by the poem or the courage it took to read it. I involuntarily clap. Then everyone joins in, and I almost start to cry—partly for her and partly for every time in the last year or two when I've felt sad or angry about my grandfather's strokes.

"Benny?" I hear. "Benny?" When I look up, Claudine has sat down and everyone is waiting for me. I skim-read my poem, knowing in my heart it's every bit as good as Claudine's, but I quickly decide not to recite it. Why? First, because my grandfather should be the first to hear it, and second, because I refuse to compete with Hobo's poem or Claudine's sadness.

Right before I'm about to break down in a classroom of seventh-grade girls and boys who will be talking about this collapse for the next twenty years, I excuse myself, grab my backpack, and leave the room, first stopping by Claudine's desk to say her poem is the "coolest" one I've ever heard. Granted, "coolest" is pretty lame, but it's hard to be creative when you're about to cry in front of your peers and a big chunk of snot is working its way out of your left nostril.

"Benny, you can't just leave class," Ms. Butterfield says. She moves toward me, but Caulfield stops her.

"I'm sorry, Ms. Butterfield," I say, "but I can. Shakespeare would understand." I don't know where the heck that comes from, but it seems appropriate.

I'm not two steps out the entrance of school when I begin to sob, and I mean "sob," not whimper or moan or shed tears, not wail or snivel. I mean a whole world of sadness comes down on me as I make my way slowly home.

ANOTHER ALVAREZ
GOES AWOL

I'd like to say it's raining outside as I begin my journey, that the sky is raven black, the wind pummeling me like the breath of an angry god—something poetic. But the weather's not cooperating with my mood. There's not a cloud in the sky, and the birds are chirping like crazy. About halfway home, I stop at a little park and sit on a swing, trying to compose myself so some passerby doesn't think I'm a nutcase and call the cops.

Two squirrels are chasing each other around an old pine tree, stopping once in a while at its base to nibble on something. Seeing as I'm not going to eat lunch today, I take two snack bags of chips from my box, slowly approaching so as not to scare them away. I crush the chips, then toss crumbs to the birds, trying to lure them toward me, remembering that day at the playground. At first they're shy, but then they creep closer, sometimes stopping to gawk, while standing on their thin legs. I wonder if they can sense my confusion. Wouldn't it be nice if they would circle and sing a song, like they did in *Sleeping Beauty*? But all I hear is my father's unhappy voice. "Another Alvarez gone AWOL," he says.

When I turn around, I'm surprised to see him smiling.

"You and Crash are going to bury me yet."

"Not appropriate, Mom would say."

"Thanks for at least choosing a playground that's on the drive to school. Otherwise, I'd be scouring the whole town."

"Is Ms. Butterfield mad?"

"No, she said to take it easy on you, that your motives were noble. I guess that poet guy spoke up for you."

"So I'm not in trouble?"

He laughs. "Well, let's see. You walk out of school in the middle of class, which I guess doesn't happen every day, and then everyone has an hour-long nervous breakdown, hoping you haven't thrown yourself into a lake or been abducted by a serial murderer."

"Only we Alvarezes think of those scenarios."

"Not according to your principal, who by the way I

should call, so he doesn't contact the police." He looks at the squirrels, who have scampered away and are hiding behind the trunk of the pine tree. "Say good-bye to your friends. You shouldn't have even gone to school today. You still look terrible."

When we arrive home, my father thaws out a container of Irene's chicken soup, and we have lunch, not saying much. He isn't mad or interested in grounding me, though after we eat, he orders me to my room. "Get some sleep," he says. Before I leave, I open my backpack and give him a copy of my poem. "Read this," I say. "It's important to me."

"Then it's important to me, too."

I can't begin to explain the weird dreams I have. There's even one where I'm at Becky Walters's party, slow dancing, yes, my friends, slow dancing with Claudine. My hands are clammy, and I'm looking over her left shoulder, trying to avoid eye contact. Surprisingly, I'm a pretty good dancer as I lead her around Becky's backyard. It's like one of my basketball dreams where I can dunk the ball.

I wake about four, feeling rested. I blow my nose for about a half hour, then shower and come downstairs. My father and Crash are playing Scrabble Junior and ask me to join them.

"That's so cool, Benny," Crash says.

"What?"

"That you walked out of school."

"Yeah, cool," my father says. "I always wanted Crash to look up to you, Benny, though I was hoping it would be for getting As on your report card."

"What Dad means, Crash, is that's it's not cool to break out of school, and if you ever do it, you better have a good reason or Mom will blame me for ruining your personality, and you're unhappy enough on your own." Though he doesn't look very unhappy as he creates a double word for ten points.

"Very nice, Crash," my father says.

We play for about fifteen minutes; then Jocko and Beanie show up. I let them in, and Jocko says, "Is your dad home? Is he mad?"

"I'm only twenty feet away, Jocko," my father says, "so you better not compare me to your mother again."

Jocko peers around the corner. "Is he serious?"

"Dead serious," my father says.

"Man, the dude has big ears."

"Yes, the dude hears everything," my father says.

Next thing I know, my father's standing behind me. I can tell by the terror in Jocko's eyes.

"Good afternoon, Mr. Alvarez," Beanie says.

"I have a question for you, Beanie. When you're with

Benny and someone shouts, 'Hey, Beanie,' how do you know they aren't saying Benny?"

Beanie's looking at him like it's a trick question.

"Ah, forget it," he says. "Why don't you guys go downstairs and I'll make some popcorn, as long as Jocko doesn't think that's effeminate."

Jocko begins to explain himself but my father interrupts, saying, "Not necessary, Jocko, not necessary at all. Just watch your back, dude."

When Crash lets out a loud laugh from the kitchen, Jocko realizes my father isn't going to whack him over the head with a poker and seal him up in a box.

In the basement, Beanie says, "What was that exit all about, dude? Everyone thinks you had a nervous breakdown."

I can't help but laugh.

"It's not funny, Benny. The guys were counting on you, and that poem is awesome."

"I was laughing at 'nervous breakdown.' What seventh grader uses that?"

"Mostly the girls," Beanie says.

"What did Ms. D and Caulfield end up doing?"

"So it's Ms. D again?" Jocko says.

"Yeah, I'm going back to it."

"Can I ask why?"

"No."

"I'm with Benny," Beanie says.

Jocko agrees, then Beanie says, "Ms. D guessed I had a copy of the poem, so she asked me to read it."

"And you did?"

"No. I knew you had your reasons for leaving."

"That must've burned Caulfield."

"The opposite. Everyone heard what you said to Claudine, and you should've seen your face. I thought you were going to hug her. Caulfield mellowed things out by saying some poems weren't meant to be read and that the contest wasn't important anymore. Finally, he gave Claudine a collection of sonnets and said he had something special for you."

"But how are you going to explain bailing to everyone else?" Jocko says.

"He doesn't have to," Beanie says. "Complimenting Claudine's poem really impressed the girls. They think you're sensitive. And guys aren't going to care about poetry in another week."

I've been called a lot of things in my life—negative, combative, confrontational—but never sensitive. I kind of like it.

"The poem is great, though," Jocko says. "You should read it."

"We'll see."

Everyone falls silent, seeing my father's feet appear on the basement stairs.

He hands me a bowl of popcorn, then walks slowly and quietly upstairs, swaying like a zombie. I should tell Beanie and Jocko he's doing this on purpose, but I don't want to ruin his fun.

"Did you see the way he looked at me?" Jocko says.

I'm trying not to laugh.

We shoot pool for a while, then I hear my mother come home, followed by her voice from the top of the stairs. "We have to talk, Benny."

"Uh-oh," Beanie and Jocko say as one, and before they leave, I thank Beanie for having my back.

"Huh?" he says.

"For not reading the poem."

"No problem, and thanks for deciding to call her Ms. D again."

"Yeah," Jocko adds, "that Butterfield is a real mouthful."

CLAUDINE AND A DOG
NOT NAMED HOBO

The next day my mother makes me stay home because she thinks my sickness caused me to weird out at the Poetry War. "People become maudlin when they're ill," she says. "Maudlin: bathetic, cornball, drippy, lachrymose, weepy." What she doesn't realize is that I knew exactly what I was doing, but fortunately, she's not mad once she discovers why I left, and I guess Ms. D and Caulfield convinced the principal not to make an example of me. My mother said the two of them were so concerned, they actually wanted to visit but then changed their minds.

Caulfield and Ms. D sipping wine in my living room? Now, that's a weird image.

I sleep late and go to breakfast with my father and Crash, who, unknown to my mother, has also called in sick. "Sometimes," my father says, "there are more important things than school."

"This coming from a teacher," I say.

"Which gives me the right to declare a holiday, Benny."

Crash couldn't care less about the logic of his day off. All he knows is he's being treated to pancakes and bacon, then later a movie. We return from the matinee early enough so I can take a nap, then I sit on the back porch, playing Scrabble Junior with Crash. We're in the final stages of Indian summer, and in spite of the rain earlier in the week, the temperature today is in the midfifties. While Crash and I are rearranging our letters, Irene and Aldo appear on the porch, Irene watching us play while Aldo fills the bird feeders.

"Grandpa's coming over tomorrow," Crash says.

"Yeah, Dad told us," I say.

"He's changed a little, Crash," Irene says, "so don't be disappointed if he's a little frail."

"We're going to watch the birds," Crash says.

"Were you listening to me?" Irene asks.

"Grandpa said to arm the Nerf gun, so we'll be able to 'come out packing.'"

Irene gives up and turns her attention to Aldo.

Just as I'm about to lay down the word "nabob," which I know Crash will unsuccessfully challenge, the doorbell rings and Spot goes crazy, even though he's heard this sound a thousand times. Irene is now helping Aldo to move a bird feeder to a safer area, and I can't locate my father, so I head for the door, hoping it's not Jocko or Beanie. I don't feel like any Benny-bailing-out-from-the-poetry-contest updates today.

I open the door, shocked to see Claudine standing before me. She looks uncomfortable, her hands behind her back. She's wearing jeans and a green fleece top, which makes her eyes seem even greener, and she's not alone. There's a tan Labrador puppy attached to a nylon leash she's obviously clutching behind her back. It's then I realize I must still be napping, so I anticipate waking or morphing into another weird fantasy, but nothing changes. Claudine's still standing there, as the puppy jerks on the leash and Spot barks and growls like a lunatic, throwing himself against the screen door.

"Is this a bad time?" she asks. When she shows her hands, one holds the leash, the other is grasping a rectangular package with blue wrapping paper and a red ribbon.

"It's always a bad time with Spot," I say. "'Weird' is probably a better word."

"Always the right word, hey, Benny?"

"What?"

"Never mind," she says, and I catch a glimpse of the old Claudine, the one who has spent the last five or six years annoyed with me.

"Spot won't do anything but lick you to death," I say, "and he loves puppies."

She laughs, the first time I've ever made her do that. The dog is jumping on her as Spot continues to yelp. Something has to be done, but I'm feeling a bit comatose.

"Why don't you ask her in?" Irene says from behind me, where she's standing with Aldo and Crash.

I open the door, and Spot immediately rushes toward the Lab, smelling its behind.

"Don't have a heart attack, Spot," I say, which is a real possibility.

Crash follows Spot, kneeling and petting the Lab, which makes Spot more excited.

"Relax, Spot," Crash says. Then he stands and scrutinizes Claudine. "Are you the harpy who's ruining Benny's life?" Unfortunately, I remember making that nasty comparison in his presence, though I doubt he even knows what it means.

"Welcome to Crazy Land," Irene says.

"You should see my house," Claudine answers.

"Don't speak too soon," Irene says. "You haven't met my father."

I can hear him climbing the basement stairs.

"Who do we have here?" he asks. He's wearing tan shorts, a black T-shirt, his winter boots, and gardening gloves. He's been cleaning his workroom and is obviously still concerned a family of mice may attack him.

"You sure you want to stay?" Irene asks Claudine.

"Yeah," Aldo says. "There's still time to reconsider, though you'll eventually get used to us all."

"I feel like I'm missing something," my father says.

"She's the harpy," Crash explains.

"Does anyone mind if I say something?" I ask, finally inviting her in. After a few introductions, everyone stands around until Irene says, "Why don't you and Benny sit on the back porch?"

"You don't mind if Happy comes, do you? He's not completely trained yet."

"Neither is Crash," my father says, patting Crash playfully on the head.

"Don't worry about it," I say. "The backyard's fenced, so the dogs can run around."

It seems like two hours before Claudine and I end up on the porch. She still looks uncomfortable.

"You're probably surprised," she says.

I'm about to reach for the Book to find the right word, because "surprised" doesn't cut it at all, but I don't want to annoy her again.

"Yeah" is all I come up with.

"I just wanted to thank you for what you said."

"I meant it. I didn't know Hobo, but I felt like I did after your poem."

"Do you think you'll read yours?"

"I want my grandfather to hear it first."

"Jocko told me."

Good old Jocko.

"I'd love to read it," she says. "All this verse poetry/prose poetry stuff seems stupid now."

"Don't expect everyone else to agree."

"Who cares? They're not the ones who wrote the poems."

"When did you get Happy?"

"The vet told my mother Hobo wouldn't get better, so she brought Happy home to keep him company, hoping she might make Hobo healthy. She didn't, but Hobo loved watching her play."

"So Happy's a girl?"

"Yeah. Pretty sappy name, isn't it?"

The sunlight is making her hair shimmer. She looks

toward Happy and Spot, who are chasing each other around a hammock. I can tell she's excited Happy is in her life, but Hobo's death still seems to weigh on her.

"I almost forgot to give you this," she says, handing me the package. "I guess Mr. Jones bought it just for you. It's a book."

I unwrap it. The title is *The Devil's Dictionary* by a guy named Ambrose Bierce.

"Mr. Jones told me to tell you, let me see," she says. "I wrote it down." Then she removes a piece of paper from her back pocket. "He said it's hundreds of definitions that are 'funny yet also true but most of all irreverent.' He said to look up any two words and read them out loud to me."

I page through the book. "Your choice: hand or history."

"Why don't you read both?"

"Hand: 'A singular instrument worn at the end of a human arm and commonly thrust into somebody's pocket.' History: 'An account, mostly false, of events, mostly unimportant, which are brought about by rulers, mostly knaves, and soldiers, mostly fools."

Claudine laughs. "I can see why he thinks they're funny."

"Yeah, but my mother would hate them."

"Why?"

"She'd think they're negative, though I'd try like heck to show her they're also true."

"You can't question everything, though, or make fun of it. It's kind of exhausting, don't you think?"

"One thing's for sure," I say, "Jocko and Beanie will like this book." Then we spend the next half hour reading some of the definitions, my favorite being, "Heaven: A place where the wicked cease from troubling you with talk of their personal affairs, and the good listen with attention while you expound your own."

Before she leaves, I go upstairs and print off a copy of my poem. I hand it to her, saying, "Don't read it until you get home."

"Sure," she says.

"And promise you won't show it to your friends, okay?"

"Promise."

There's an uncomfortable silence, because we both know the rules have suddenly changed. Like me, she's probably wondering how we'll deal with each other from now on, because kids are used to us arguing.

After she's gone, Crash joins me on the porch. "Sorry the harpy thing slipped out. I knew it was a lousy word because I looked it up after you used it."

"What did you find?"

"It's a filthy, hungry monster with the head of a woman

and a bird's body. Don't know why you ever called her
that, Benny."

"Doesn't quite fit her, does it?"

"No, she's pretty."

"Yeah, everyone says that."

"Cool dog, too."

RETURN OF THE HAWK

It's late Wednesday afternoon, and the sun's beginning to slide behind two huge oak trees in our backyard. My grandfather and I are alone on the porch. He still looks tired and has a tendency to stare into the distance at something only he can see. It took us about five minutes to get him from the car to the porch. He and Crash sat for a while, then my father took Crash to play miniature golf, so my grandfather and I could be alone.

He has the plaid shawl around his shoulders and his hands folded on his lap, and we're watching a cardinal peck away at one of the bird feeders. Then a few squirrels come along, managing to climb the cast-iron pole. They hang upside down from the feeder, gorging themselves.

"They're not supposed to be able to do that, are they?" my grandfather says.

"No, Grandpa." I leave him for a second and grab a can of lubricant Aldo bought. I chase the squirrels off the feeder, then spray the pole and rejoin my grandfather. We watch as the squirrels attempt to climb the bird feeder again, this time unable to grasp it, sliding onto shrubbery below. They try again with the same result.

"Good for them," my grandfather says. "You ever eat a squirrel?"

"Can't say I have, Grandpa."

"Better than you might think if cooked properly."

"I wrote you a poem."

"A poem?"

"Well, it's really a prose poem."

"What's that?"

"It's hard to explain."

"Then don't. I have enough trouble with simple things."

And so I recite my poem for the very first time.

"Will you read it again?" he says. "I missed a few parts."

And I do.

He smiles. "Never been the subject of a poem before, especially one written by an Alvarez."

"You like it?"

He takes off his glasses, and when he rubs the bridge of

his nose, I see a few tears, so I place my hands on his.

"It's my life, isn't it, some of the things that make a man?"

"It's what I see when I think of you."

"It's pretty ac—" and he can't find the word.

"Accurate?"

He's about to reply but then points above. A hawk is circling, and I'm hoping it's not the same one Crash saw snatch a bird. Aldo said that when a hawk knows where to feed, it returns.

"Where'd Crash go?" my grandfather asks.

"Out with Dad."

"Good. I have a feeling that bird has his eye on us." When he says this, the hawk drops, resting on a thick oak branch, no more than fifty feet from the bird feeders. He's a beautiful creature, and crafty because he pretends to ignore us while sizing up his meal. Suddenly we hear the whoosh of his wings flapping, but instead of attacking the bird feeder, he rises up into the sky, circling a few times, then disappearing from sight.

"He won't be back," my grandfather says.

"How do you know, Grandpa?"

"Because I told him to leave us alone. I'm not ready yet."

"For what?"

He doesn't answer, but instead says, "Will you slide that poem into my pocket?"

"Sure, Grandpa," I say, folding the poem and doing as he asks.

We sit quietly for a moment, then I read him excerpts from *The Devil's Dictionary*, which make him laugh.

"It's funny how people think, isn't it?"

"Yeah, Grandpa. Can I get you some hot cider?"

"Sure," he says.

As I heat the cider in a small saucepan, he watches the birds peck at the feeders. Then he manages to reach inside his pocket for my poem. He can't read it, so he runs his hands slowly over the paper, removing his glasses again and wiping his eyes dry.

I think of the hawk, circling over another location by now, and I marvel at its cool detachment, though I'm also saddened for the creatures it preys upon.

And for now, I'm glad it's gone.

PETER JOHNSON

grew up in Buffalo, New York, at a time when they had a good football team, which seems like fifty years ago. Similar to Benny Alvarez and his friends, Peter always loved words, knowing he was going to be a teacher or a professional baseball player. Also, being from a long line of Irish storytellers, he loved reading and telling tales, and when he realized that his stories changed every time he told them, and that he could get paid for this kind of lying, he decided to become a novelist. His first middle-grade novel, *The Amazing Adventures of John Smith, Jr. AKA Houdini*, was named one of the Best Children's Books by *Kirkus Reviews*, and he's received many writing fellowships, most notably from the National Endowment for the Arts. You can find him at www.peterjohnsonya.com.